Her mind drifted to the image she had once had of him—Maximilian Hart, the powerful, ruthless, intimidating mover and shaker who always got what he wanted.

The master player. He'd moved her, shaken the whole foundation of her world, but what, in the end, did he want with her?

Right now, Chloe couldn't bring herself to care.

She loved being with him like this.

And she was going to revel in it as long as it lasted.

Dear Reader,

The Master Player is my 100th romance. I know there are some of you who have read every one of them. What an amazing journey we have shared! I wonder if my most fondly remembered stories over this span of twenty-six years are the same as yours….

The Wrong Mirror and *Merry Christmas* for their sheer life drama—I wept many tears living those situations.

My first sheikh book, *The Falcon's Mistress*—so wonderfully exotic—and *The Secret Mistress*—huge drama in South America with my one Argentinean hero.

The Upstairs Lover and *Jack's Baby*—for the sheer fun in them.

Bride of His Choice and THE OUTBACK KNIGHTS KINGS trilogy—very strong stories driven by family history as so many lives are.

But my all-time favorite is *Their Wedding Day*— a magnificent hero who slays all the heroine's dragons and is the perfect father—a fairy-tale prince in their minds—for the children who have been deserted by her husband.

Because I loved this story so much, I wanted to choose another wonderfully masterful hero and a similar theme—the white knight to the rescue—for my 100th book. I do hope you enjoy it.

It has been the longest pleasure of my life, being a romance author—like being a fairy godmother who can wave a magic wand and make everything turn out right—and I want to thank you, my readers, for making it possible.

With love always,

Emma Darcy

Emma Darcy
THE MASTER PLAYER

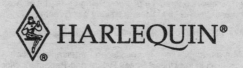

HARLEQUIN®

TORONTO • NEW YORK • LONDON
AMSTERDAM • PARIS • SYDNEY • HAMBURG
STOCKHOLM • ATHENS • TOKYO • MILAN • MADRID
PRAGUE • WARSAW • BUDAPEST • AUCKLAND

Recycling programs
for this product may
not exist in your area.

ISBN-13: 978-0-373-12878-5

THE MASTER PLAYER

First North American Publication 2009.

Copyright © 2009 by Emma Darcy.

www.eHarlequin.com

Printed in U.S.A.

All about the author...
Emma Darcy

EMMA DARCY was born in Australia, and currently lives on a beautiful country property in New South Wales, she has moved from country to city to towns and back to country, sporadically indulging her love of tropical islands with numerous vacations.

Her ambition to be an actress was partly satisfied when she played in amateur theater productions, but ultimately fulfilled when she became a writer. Initially a teacher of French and English, she changed her career to computer programming before marriage and motherhood settled her into community life. Her creative urges were channeled into oil painting, pottery, and designing and overseeing the construction and decorating of two homes, all in the midst of keeping up with three lively sons and the very busy social life of her businessman husband.

A voracious reader, the step to writing her own books seemed a natural progression to Emma, and the challenge of creating wonderful stories was soon highly addictive. With her strong interest in people and relationships, Emma found the world of romance fiction a happy one.

Currently she has broadened her horizons and begun to write mainstream women's fiction. Other new directions include her most recent adventures of blissfully breezing around the Gulf of Mexico from Florida to Louisiana in a red convertible, and risking the perils of the tortuous road along the magnificent Amalfi Coast in Italy.

Her conviction that we must make all we can out of the life we are given keeps her striving to know more, be more and give more, and this is reflected in all her books.

I dedicate this book to all the readers who have traveled through my worlds and shared the smiles and the tears with me.

CHAPTER ONE

HE watched her. The launch party for the new hit television show was packed with celebrities, many of the women more structurally beautiful than the one he watched, but to Maximilian Hart's mind, she outshone them all. There was a lovely simplicity about her that attracted both men and women, a natural quality that evoked the sense she would never play anyone false. The quintessential girl next door whom everyone liked and trusted, Max thought, plus the soft sensuality in her femininity that made every man want to go to bed with her.

There was nothing hard, nothing intimidating about the way she looked. Her blonde hair was in a soft short flyaway style that invariably seemed slightly ruffled, not sprayed into shape. There were dimples in her cheeks when she smiled. Her face had no sharp lines. Even her nose ended in a soft tilt. And her body was how a woman's should be—no bony shoulders, no sticklike arms, every part of her sweetly rounded and curved, not voluptuously so, not threatening to other women but very inviting to any man.

Though her eyes were the real key to her attraction, their luminous light blue colour somehow suggested that her soul was open for listening to and empathising with anything you wanted to tell her. Nothing guarded about those eyes. They drew you in, showing every emotion, transmitting an almost mesmerising vulnerability that stirred a man's protective instincts as well as the more basic ones.

The wide generous mouth was almost as expressive as the eyes, its soft mobility reflecting the same feelings from a grimace of sympathy to a scintillating smile of shared joy. She had the gift of projecting whatever you wanted from her and you believed she truly felt it, not an actress playing a part. It was a gift that could turn her into a huge star, and not just in the television show he'd bought and had rewritten to showcase what he'd seen in her.

Oddly enough, he wasn't sure she wanted to be one. Her domineering mother wanted it. Her ambitious script-writer husband wanted it. She did what *they* wanted, never raising any objection to it but there had been occasions when Max had glimpsed a lost look on her face—moments when she thought no-one was watching, when she wasn't required to be someone else's creation, when she was not *on show*.

She was on show tonight and the party people were flocking to her, wanting to share her spotlight, fascinated by her unique charisma whether they wanted to be or not. The crowd around her kept shifting, changing, forced to give way to others who wanted a piece of her if only for a little while. Although Max noted that those most closely connected to her life left her to shine alone.

It didn't surprise him. Neither her mother nor her husband enjoyed the role of background person, which they inevitably became if they attached themselves to her in public. He tore his gaze away from her to glance around, unsurprised when he spotted her mother schmoozing up to a group of television executives, increasing her network of contacts she could use. Max had disliked dealing with her. Unavoidable since she had appointed herself her daughter's agent. He kept any business meeting with her short and coldly rebuffed any attempt at a more personal connection with him.

Pushy, full of her own ego, Stephanie Rollins was the worst kind of stage-mother. Her vividly dyed carrot-red hair yelled *notice me, remember me,* even without its butch shortness, which accentuated her abrasive attitude of *I'm as good as any man and better than most.* Though there was nothing butch about her body, which she dressed with in-your-face sexiness; cleavage on show, tight skirts, extremely high heels to bring attention to her shapely legs.

Everything was used as a weapon in her fight to win her own way and there was nothing Max liked about her. Even the name she'd chosen for her daughter—Chloe—seemed deliberately artful, aimed at being remembered. Chloe Rollins. It rolled off the tongue, yet it always struck a false note with Max. It seemed too contrived for the person he saw in Chloe. Something simple would have suited her better.

Mary.

Mary Hart.

His mouth twitched with amusement at the fanciful addition of his own surname. Marriage had never appealed to him. He didn't want a wife. Sexual urges were satisfied with one woman or another and his butler and cook did everything else a wife could do. Besides, Chloe Rollins already had a husband and Max didn't believe in poaching other men's wives, not even for a casual affair. Having a messy private life had no more appeal than having a messy business life. Max stayed firmly in control of both.

He wondered what use her husband was making of this party and his gaze roved around the crowd, seeking the handsome charmer Chloe had married, Tony Lipton. *He* was well named. The guy was full of glib lip but Max didn't think much of his writing ability. None of the lines he came up with had any emotional punch. They invariably had to be edited, sharpened by other writers on the script-writing team for the show. Tony Lipton wouldn't be on the team at all but for his inclusion in the deal with Chloe.

Interesting…he was not currying attention. He was right off at the edge of the party crowd, half-turned away from it and having what looked like a very tense exchange with Chloe's personal assistant, Laura Farrell. Angry frustration on his face. Angry determination on hers. Tony grabbed her arm, fingers digging in with a viselike grip. She wrenched herself free of it and whirled away from him, her face set in seething resentment as she barged through the crowd, making a beeline for Chloe.

Max's instinct for trouble was instantly alerted. There were media people here. He did not subscribe to the view that any publicity—however bad—was good publicity. Any distraction from the success of the show was not welcome, particularly anything unpleasant centred on the star.

He moved, carving his own way through the crowd, but he was coming from the opposite side of the room—impossible to intercept Laura. She reached Chloe first, shoving past the cluster of people surrounding her, moving into a stance of close confrontation, her body language screaming fierce purpose, her hands curling around Chloe's shoulders as she leaned forward and whispered something venomous.

Definitely venomous.

The shock on Chloe's face—the totally stricken look—told

Max this was big trouble. Fortunately he was only a few seconds behind Laura, close enough for his tall and power-fully built physique to shield that look from most of the nearby spectators.

'Get out of my way, Laura,' he commanded, the steely tone of his voice startling the woman into releasing Chloe and swinging around to face him.

He moved swiftly, cutting straight past her, curling an arm around Chloe's waist, scooping her close to his side, walking her away from the source of her distress, his head bent towards her, talking intently as though he had something important to impart, his free arm held out in a warding-off gesture that would deter anyone from interrupting the tête-à-tête.

'Don't make any fuss,' he dictated in a low urgent voice. 'Just come with me and I'll take you to a safe place where we can deal with this problem in private.'

She didn't respond. She stared blankly ahead and walked like an automaton, carried forward by the force of his momen-tum. It was as if she had suddenly become a shell of a person with nothing going on inside. Max reasoned that whatever Laura had told her had to have been one hell of a shock to reduce her to this state.

His immediate aim was to protect her, protect his investment in her, and he did it as ruthlessly as he went after anything he targeted. He didn't care what her mother or her husband thought of his action. He steered her straight out of the Starlight Room—the premier function room in this five-star hotel—ignoring calls for his attention, quelling any pursuit of them with a forbidding look. No-one wanted to get on the wrong side of Australia's television baron. He had too much power to cross, and Max had no scruples about using it as it suited him.

He'd booked the penthouse suite for his convenience tonight. Wanting to enjoy his own private satisfaction in Chloe Rollins, he hadn't invited his current mistress to the party so there was no risk of any acrimonious scene if he took Chloe there. It provided a quick and effective escape for her.

He didn't bother asking for her consent. She wasn't hearing anything. Didn't seem to be aware of anything, either. There was no word or sign of protest from her as he led her into an elevator, rode up to the top floor, escorted her into his suite, locked the door behind them and saw her seated in a comfortable armchair.

She did not relax against the soft cushions. Max wasn't sure she even knew she was sitting down. He moved to the bar and poured a generous measure of brandy into one of the balloon glasses provided. He poured himself a Scotch, intent on appearing companionable rather than intimidating, when the brandy jolted her back to life.

She wasn't comfortable with him, never had been. He didn't set out to charm people and was probably too forceful a personality for her to easily like. But right now he was the man in charge and he wanted her to accept that situation, give him her trust, confide the problem and let him resolve it because clearly she was incapable of dealing with it herself and he needed his star actress to keep performing as only she could. Maximilian Hart did not take losses on any project he engineered.

'Drink this!'

A large balloon glass was shoved forcefully at the hands lying listlessly in her lap. Her dulled mind registered that she had to take it or it would tip over and spill its contents. She wrapped both hands around it to hold it steady.

'Drink!'

The hard command rattled her into lifting the glass to her lips. She sipped and liquid fire seared her palate and burned a path down her throat. Heat scorched up her neck, flooded into her cheeks and zapped her brain out of its numbed state. Eyes filled with pained protest automatically targeted the man who had made this happen.

Maximilian Hart.

A shudder ran through her at the realisation that *he* was standing over her, the power that always emanated from him kicking into her heart and causing her stomach muscles to contract.

'That's better,' he said, satisfaction glinting in the dark eyes that shone with too much brilliant intelligence, invariably giving her the impression that nothing could be hidden from him. He'd seen it all, knew it all, and cared only for what advantage it could give him in the world he was master of.

It was a relief when he turned away from her, putting physical distance between them as he strolled over to the armchair facing hers on the other side of a sofa and a glass coffee table, which was placed to serve any occupants of the lounge suite. He sat down, folding his long, strong body into the chair, his elegant hands casually nursing a drink of his own.

He was a strikingly handsome man, though that was a totally inadequate description of him. The dark good looks—black hair, strongly chiselled face, deeply set brown eyes, tanned skin, perfectly sculptured mouth—added to his air of distinction, but it was the aura of indomitable power that gave him a charismatic impact, which made all the rest seem merely a fitting outer framework for the dynamic person who could take over anything and make it work.

Somehow it heightened his sexuality, almost to the point of mental and physical assault on everything that was female in Chloe. She wanted to recoil from it, yet could not switch off the magnetism he exerted, tugging out feelings she shouldn't have with this man. It was alarming to find herself alone with him.

Her gaze jerked around, taking in what was obviously an executive suite. With a king-size bed. Which instantly reminded her of the one Tony had insisted they buy for their bedroom.

Had he used it with Laura?

Is that where he'd so carelessly committed the worst betrayal of all?

'What did Laura Farrell tell you?'

The question pulled her gaze back to Maximilian Hart, forcing her to meet his riveting dark eyes—no escape from telling him the truth. She could feel the pressure of his willpower pounding on her mind and knew he wouldn't tolerate any evasion. Besides, it couldn't be covered up. Laura didn't want it covered up. And neither did she. No argument in the world could make her resume her marriage after this.

'She's been having an affair with my husband.' A double betrayal—a woman she'd trusted as a friend and the man who'd pretended to love her. 'She's pregnant...carrying his child.' The child Tony had denied her because this new television show was too big an opportunity to pass up. Her mouth wobbled at having to speak the final sickening words. 'He won't leave me for her because I'm...I'm his cash cow.'

She closed her eyes as bitter tears welled into them.

'He certainly won't want to leave you,' came the cynical comment. 'The critical question is...will you leave him?'

A huge anger erupted through her, cracking open a mountain of old wounds she had buried in getting on with the life her mother had pushed her into from infancy onwards, cutting off other options, leaving her no choice but to follow the path set down for her. Her marriage to Tony was part of that…the baby she'd been talked out of having. *No more, no more, no more,* screamed through her mind.

She dashed away the tears with the back of her hand and glared at the man who was querying her response to the situation. 'Yes,' she answered vehemently. 'I won't let you or Tony or my mother sweep this under the mat. I don't care if it hurts my image. I'll never take him back as my husband.'

'Fine!' he said with a casual gesture of dismissal. 'I just wanted to know how best to deal with the situation, given our abrupt departure from the Starlight Room.'

'I won't go back there, either,' she threw at him in full-blown rebellion. 'I don't want to see or talk to Tony or be anywhere near him. Nor do I want to listen to my mother.'

He regarded her thoughtfully for several moments, the powerful dark eyes probing, assessing, speculating, making her feel like a butterfly on a pin being minutely examined. She wrenched her gaze away from his and took a gulp of brandy, wanting its fire to burn away the humiliation of being nothing but a cash cow to the people who had brought her to this.

Maximilian Hart was no different, she savagely told herself. He only cared about her because of the huge investment he'd made in the television show, redesigning it as a vehicle for what he perceived as her special talent. Whatever *that* was. Though she was grateful to him for getting her out of the Starlight Room. She couldn't remember him doing it but he'd obviously observed the impact of Laura's revelation and acted to minimise its effect on the launch party.

The show must go on.

But not tonight.

Not for her.

'Since you don't wish to be reached by your very tenacious mother, nor your husband, who will undoubtedly be plotting how to dump this on Laura Farrell and make himself out to be the innocent victim of a woman deranged with jealousy…' He paused a moment watching for her reaction to that scenario.

Chloe was rattled by it.

'Which, I assure you, would be a lie,' he went on sardonically. 'I observed them in very intimate conversation together just prior to her assault on you. She was furious with him. The connection between them was not fantasy.'

'The baby would prove it anyway,' she muttered bitterly.

'Not if Laura is persuaded to have an abortion.'

Chloe looked at him in horror.

He shook his head. 'Not by me.'

Tony. And her mother. She knew without him telling her they would both see that as a way out of an unsavoury scandal, a way of smoothing everything over so she would keep going as they directed. Her head started to throb at the thought of all the arguments they would subject her to.

'I've got to get away from them. Got to…' She was barely aware of saying the words out loud. Her mind was desperately seeking some way of escape, but everything she had was tied up with Tony and her mother…her money, her home, her whole life.

'I can protect you, Chloe.'

Startled by a claim she had not been expecting, she stared at him in anguished confusion. The look of arrogant confidence on his face reminded her of how powerful he was. The dark eyes bored into hers with a relentless strength that set all her nerves twittering. Of course, Maximilian Hart could protect her if he wanted to. But what would that mean?

'You need to move to a safe refuge where the security is so tight no-one can reach you unless you want them to,' he said matter-of-factly. 'It's no problem to me to arrange that.'

A peaceful haven, sheer heaven, she thought, though practical issues instantly raised difficulties. 'I'd have to go home to get my clothes.'

'No. Professional movers can pack and deliver them to you.'

'I don't even have my credit card with me.'

'I'll put a lawyer to work sorting out your financial situation. In the meantime I'll set up a bank account for you that will cover your needs until you're in charge of your own money.'

She winced. 'My mother will fight to keep control.'

'I doubt she has more weapons than I have,' he drawled, ruthless intent gleaming in the brilliant dark eyes.

He was right.

Her mother was no match for him.

Freedom shimmered in front of her.

'Trust me, Chloe. There is nothing I can't do to set you on an independent path. *If* that is what you want.'

Seductive words, pulling her his way. *Yes* teetered on the tip of her tongue. Only the sudden sharp sense that she'd be walking out of one form of possession straight into another held it back.

'Why would you do this for me?' The words tumbled out on a wave of fear—fear that he meant to mould her into what *he* wanted, and the promise of independence was the lure to trap her into something worse than she had known.

'I don't want any disruption to the delivery of this show, which has been—and is—a project I've planned for a very long time. You're the key player in it, Chloe. I need you functioning as only you can. If that means freeing you of every distressing influence, ensuring you won't be got at by people who'll cause you grief, I'll do it. Throw a blanket of security around you that no-one can break without your permission. All I ask in return is that you keep working on the show for as long as your contract runs.'

Protecting his investment.

It made sense.

Maximilian Hart was always linked to success, never failure.

This wasn't a personal thing to him. It was business. He simply didn't want her private life adversely affecting what he had put in place.

Her fears suddenly seemed ludicrous. Strangely enough, she felt a surge of confidence that she could do as he asked—keep playing her part in the show—if she didn't have to deal with her mother or Tony or Laura while she did it.

'I'll make them go away,' he said softly, somehow tapping straight into her thoughts. 'Just say the word, Chloe.'

Her battered mind started swimming with a vision of a white knight fighting all her dragons instead of a dangerous Svengali of a man planning to use her for some devious purpose of his own. It was more than seductive. It propelled her into accepting his offer without any further fretting over it.

'It *is* what I want,' spilled from her lips.

'Yes,' he said as though he'd known it all along and had only been waiting for her to confirm it. He rose from his chair with the air of a man relishing the sniff of battle. 'You'll be absolutely safe waiting for me here. You probably need to eat something. Order whatever you like from room service. Make yourself comfortable and relax, knowing you don't have to face harassment from any source tonight.'

'Where are you going?'

'Back to the Starlight Room.' He smiled a smile of intense private satisfaction. 'By the time I've finished there, I doubt anyone will have the desire to harass you about your decision.'

Her decision.

An independent decision.

She felt weirdly awed by it as she watched the man who'd made it so easily possible walk away to begin putting it into effect. Maximilian Hart. Who had the power to do whatever he set out to do. And he was about to use his power to free her from the life she'd wanted to escape from for as long as she could remember.

CHAPTER TWO

'WHAT'S going on, Max?'

The question was shot at him the moment he re-entered the Starlight Room—it was Lisa Cox, the editor for the entertainment section in one of the major newspapers, sniffing a story that might have more sensational value than a report on a launch party and waiting to pounce on the major source for it. She was a sharp-faced woman with big curly hair, inquisitive eyes and a dangerous tongue.

'You whip out of here with Chloe, who looked like death,' she swiftly put in. 'You come back alone...'

'Chloe is resting,' he blandly stated.

'What's wrong with her?'

'The energy drain of the party, continually responding to people without pausing to eat or drink. I think she needed a fast sugar-hit,' he said with a frown of concern.

'Does she have diabetes?'

'I'm about to speak to her mother about Chloe's condition, if you'll excuse me.'

He stepped aside, his gaze already scanning the crowd for a carrot-red head.

'Is this going to be a problem for the show?' Lisa threw at him.

He returned a freezing-off smile. 'No. Someone needs to take better care of her. That's all. And I'll make sure it's done.'

Closure on that issue. No gossip to pursue.

Stephanie Rollins had moved to the far corner of the room, obviously involved in a heated discussion with Tony Lipton and Laura Farrell. They were unaware of his return, probably the only three people in the room who were since the crowd literally parted to make way for him as he took the most direct path to where they stood.

Laura Farrell was tall, model-slim, straight brown hair falling to her shoulder blades, wearing an elegant black dress, in keeping with her personal style of always appearing in good classic clothes. She had amber eyes—cat's eyes. Max had seen envy in them when she was looking at Chloe. Contempt, as well. As though Chloe was stupid and didn't deserve her status as a star.

It was a completely different story when Chloe was looking at her—sweetly helpful, indulgently helpful, happy to do whatever was asked of her. The two-faced bitch had shown her true colours tonight. Max was looking forward to banishing her from Chloe's orbit.

Tony Lipton, as well, even more so, the smarmy con man riding his gravy train without any real caring for the woman who'd been carrying him. With his streaky blond hair and green eyes he could almost be a clone for Robert Redford in his prime, but his only talent was for looking good and talking himself up. The fall is coming, Max silently promised him as Tony caught sight of his approach, was visibly alarmed by it and quickly warned the others.

The two women sprang aside, automatically making room for him to join the group. Laura's face held a mixture of fear and belligerence. She had to know she'd dug her own grave as Chloe's personal assistant but she was going to fight to come out on top with a hefty slice of Chloe's wealth through Tony's mistake in getting her pregnant. No doubt she'd get long-term support out of his divorce settlement. The pregnancy would not have been a mistake on her part.

There was tight-lipped anger on Stephanie's face. She'd obviously been counting the cost of the inevitable fallout and didn't like the score. She'd like it even less when he slapped her with Chloe's total disaffection from her domination.

The tension amongst the group was palpable, waiting for him to present them with a platform from which to push their hotly contesting barrows. Max wasn't about to give it to them in full view of interested spectators.

'No doubt you're all concerned about Chloe,' he said, barely keeping an acid sarcasm out of his voice. 'I've taken her to a private suite. I suggest you all accompany me out of here so the situation can be discussed in private. I urge you not to speak to anyone as we go. You won't like the consequences if you do.'

'You can't do anything to me,' Laura jeered defiantly.

'Shut your bloody mouth!' Tony sliced at her.

'Take my arm, Stephanie,' Max commanded, holding it out for public linkage to Chloe's mother.

No hesitation there.

Max shot a steely look at the gravy-train specialist. 'Follow us, Tony, and bring your woman with you.'

The perfect golden tan on his face didn't look so perfect stained with a guilty red flush, but Max didn't pause to take pleasure in the effect. He retraced his path across the room with Stephanie Rollins in tow, his head bent to her in a pose of confidential conversation, murmuring a string of platitudes about the need to look after Chloe more carefully.

It only took a matter of minutes to have the three of them away from the party and in an elevator being whisked up to what they undoubtedly expected to be a showdown with Chloe. On the executive floor he led them to a door where a butler was standing, ready to let them in and hand over the pass card to Max, who had arranged for this second suite to be available on his way down from the one Chloe was now occupying.

They trooped in.

He closed the door.

Stephanie was the first to react. 'Where's Chloe?' she snapped, eyes suspicious of having been maneuvred into a place that held no advantage to her.

'Where she wants to be…out of reach from any of you,' he replied, sweeping all three of them with a look of icy contempt before addressing Stephanie. 'Since you hired Laura Farrell as Chloe's personal assistant, I suggest you now fire her. She will not be welcome anywhere near Chloe again. Is that understood, Stephanie?'

She nodded, too smart to argue against what he was telling her point-blank was unfixable.

'I wouldn't work for her again anyway,' Laura mumbled.

Max ignored her, targeting Tony next. 'You're fired from the script-writing team.'

'You can't do that. I've got a contract,' he spluttered.

'I'll buy it out. My lawyer will be in touch with you to settle. Consider the contract terminated as of now. I don't want you anywhere in the vicinity of Chloe when she's working on the show.'

'But…'

'Go quietly, Tony,' he advised, threat underlining every word as he added, 'I could have you blacklisted from the whole television industry.'

'For God's sake! I just made a mistake in my private life. It has nothing to do with my profession,' he protested.

'It's not private when it affects my business. Go quietly, Tony,' he repeated.

He shook his head in shattered disbelief that his dalliance with Laura Farrell would bring such fast and comprehensive reprisal—banished from the golden star circle, in danger of being completely exiled from celebrity stamping grounds, and without Chloe at his side he had no leverage to change what was being dealt out to him.

Satisfied that Tony was now fully aware of consequences, Max turned his attention back to Chloe's mother. His strong inclination was to get rid of her altogether, but family bonds were tricky. Without consulting further with Chloe, he had to check himself on that front.

'I don't believe you've acted in your daughter's best interests, Stephanie, which you should have done both as her mother and her agent.'

'This is none of my doing,' she cried, one hand flying out in a cutting dismissal of Laura and Tony.

'You chose Laura and you allowed Tony to attach himself to Chloe's career. Bad judgement on both counts,' Max bored in relentlessly. 'You will meet with me at eleven o'clock tomorrow morning in my city office for a discussion on whether or not you will continue to be her agent.'

'That's between me and Chloe,' she vehemently argued.

'No. She has given me the power to act on her behalf and

I shall, Stephanie. Believe me, I shall. You might want to bring a lawyer with you. Mine will certainly be there.'

'Let me talk to her,' came the swift demand, a flicker of fear behind the calculation in her eyes. 'We've got too much history for you to interfere like this.'

'Chloe does not want to listen to you,' Max stated unequivocally, pushing the position through with calm ruthlessness. 'I suggest you accept that your domination of your daughter is over and your best course is to move into damage control rather than try fighting me. I am a very formidable opponent, Stephanie.'

He left that threat hanging for several moments, letting it sink in before announcing, 'I will now leave you to return to the Starlight Room. None of you will be allowed back into it tonight. The butler will evict you from this suite in thirty minutes. A prompt exit from the hotel would be your wisest move.'

He turned his back on them, let himself out of the suite, gave the butler his instructions, then, not anticipating any pursuit from the group he'd left to contemplate their future, he took an elevator down to the function room floor and rejoined the party in the Starlight Room.

Lisa Cox caught hold of him and inquired, 'Chloe not returning?'

'No. She's been on a publicity treadmill this past week and needs a rest from it,' he said in casual dismissal. 'Why not chat to some of the other cast members, Lisa? I'm sure they'd all be happy to give you their view of the show.'

He smiled to wipe out the concern he'd displayed earlier and moved off to do some mixing with the cast himself, making his presence felt at the party for the next forty minutes, which was long enough to publicly distance himself from

Chloe's absence and long enough for the unholy trio to have made their departure from the hotel.

Then excusing himself on the grounds of celebration fatigue, he made a show of retiring for the night, returned to the executive floor, checked that the second suite he'd acquired was empty, then continued on to the one where he'd left Chloe. Only a little over an hour had passed since she'd made her decision. If she'd developed cold feet about it, he'd have to convince her there was no going back. Actions had already been taken.

She belonged with him now.

The thought jolted him, carrying with it as it did an immense satisfaction. It was too strong, smacking of a possessiveness that was alien to him where women were concerned. In maintaining his own freedom he'd always respected their freedom to make their own choices, as well. But he did own Chloe Rollins in a professional sense, for the duration of her contract with him, and she was now free in a personal sense, giving him the opportunity to pursue his interest in her. That was what was giving him this extra buzz of excitement.

She was the most fascinating woman he'd ever met and she was no longer tied to her husband. He could take her, keep her with him, explore the woman she was inside and out, for as long as he wanted to.

Chloe had not moved from the armchair where Max had left her. A review of her life had been churning through her mind—the whole horrible hollowness of being more important to her mother as an image on a television screen than a person with real needs that were ignored or dismissed.

She'd fallen in love with Tony because he'd seemed to

focus entirely on her, the woman, making her feel truly loved, caring about what she wanted. All pretence. No sooner were they married than he'd started allying himself with her mother, adding to the pressure to maintain the image on the screen, sugar-coating it by telling her how special she was.

She'd fallen out of love with him very quickly, disillusioned by how he manipulated their life together to his liking, not hers, but he'd been easier to live with than her mother so she'd done whatever he'd required of her to make the relationship harmonious enough, even to this last deal with Maximilian Hart—Tony angling to be part of the script-writing team, arguing that he could share the show with her, be on hand to look after her interests, ensure she had everything she wanted.

Lies.

All lies.

He'd spent more time with Laura than with her, bedding Laura, getting Laura pregnant, while still pretending to be a loving husband. Not that she'd believed it anymore. He loved her career, the contacts, the celebrity whirl. She was the vehicle for the life he wanted, the life her mother wanted.

The marriage had felt empty long before this. Which was why she'd wanted a baby. A baby's love would have been real and she would have loved it so much. So very much. A child of her own to do everything right for.

Chloe had kept sipping the brandy, liking the fire in her belly. It made her feel alive, made her feel more determined to take charge of her life once this contract with Maximilian Hart had been fulfilled. It felt good to have him on her side, knowing he would help her get through this huge change in her life. It made perfect sense that he didn't want her so encumbered by problems that she couldn't shine in his show. She understood that a man like him would want this project to fulfil the potential he'd envisaged. While it was true she was a key player in making that happen, Maximilian Hart was the master player, orchestrating whatever was needed to achieve the desired success.

A man like him...

The phrase had slid through her mind. She tried to analyse what it meant and all she could come up with was a sense of absolute control of himself and everything he did. Maximilian Hart exuded power. Was that what gave him the sexual magnetism that invariably rattled her? It probably rattled every woman who was subjected to his presence.

Chloe was totally unaware of time passing. Hearing the door to the suite being opened jolted her into leaping out of the armchair and turning to face the man who'd done whatever he'd done to ensure she was free of harassment. That was much easier to accept when he was not here. The moment Maximilian Hart came into view, her heart started skittering with nervous apprehension.

'It's all right,' he instantly assured her. 'You won't have to see any of them again unless you wish to.' His gaze dropped to the empty balloon glass she was still nursing in her hands, then quickly swung around the tables in the room. 'You haven't eaten?'

'No. I...' She flushed, remembering his instructions to order something from room service. 'I just didn't think of it.'

He smiled reassuringly. 'You don't have to if you don't want to, Chloe. I'm feeling somewhat peckish myself, so I'm going to order us club sandwiches, which you can eat or not as you please.'

She watched him move to the writing desk, pick up the telephone, speak to room service. He added French fries to the order, then asked her, 'Tea, coffee or hot chocolate?'

'Hot chocolate. And tomato sauce.'

He raised a quizzical eyebrow.

'I like tomato sauce with French fries,' she explained, not caring if it sounded childish. She suddenly felt peckish, too, and wanted to enjoy the food he'd ordered.

His smile was one of satisfaction this time. Chloe wished his smiles would make him less daunting but they didn't. They gave her the sense he was one move ahead of her and they were designed to make her feel better about falling in with him. He was probably ten moves ahead of her. She needed to get her wits together and find out what he'd done on her behalf.

Having completed the room service order, he wrote something on the notepad beside the telephone. 'I've booked another suite for myself and stopped all calls to this one so you're assured of an uninterrupted night. When you're ready for breakfast tomorrow morning, call me on this number—' he tapped the notepad '—and I'll join you to plot out the next steps that have to be taken. Okay?'

She nodded, relieved to know he wasn't thinking of spending the night with her. Not that she had worried about that in any sexual sense. It was a well-known fact he was currently connected to the model Shannah Lian, a gorgeous redhead who oozed class. While Shannah had not attended the party with him tonight, probably because of some other commitment, Chloe didn't connect the model's absence to any interest Maximilian Hart might have in herself.

This was business for him. However, he might have

thought she shouldn't be left alone, and the simple truth was she couldn't relax in his presence. Her gaze drifted to the bed. It would be good to climb into it, knowing she was alone. A shudder of revulsion ran through her at the thought of Tony having sex with her after he'd been with Laura. Never again!

'Tony will not be connected to the show anymore, Chloe. I've fired him from the script-writing team. Laura Farrell will be gone, as well. They're both out of your professional life.'

Clearing the set for the show to go on, Chloe thought, but their banishment did give her a vengeful satisfaction. 'Good!' she said, swinging her gaze back to the man who'd used his power to free her from them in the workplace. 'Thank you.'

He strolled towards her, gesturing towards the armchair she had vacated. 'Room service will take a while and we need to talk about your mother.'

She sat down, seething with rebellion against anything her mother might have suggested to him, ready to fight any continuance of the control that had blighted her life. He took his time, settling in his armchair, the dark eyes observing her edginess, making her feel even more tense.

'Do you want to keep her as your agent?' he asked.

'No.' The word exploded from a mountain of resentments. A rush of doubts followed it. She had no idea of the legalities of the situation. 'Do I have to?'

He shook his head. 'I took the liberty of arranging a meeting with her tomorrow for the purpose of ending the business relationship between you.'

He'd already taken the initiative! Chloe stared at him in awed silence.

He made an offhand gesture. 'You still have the choice.'

'I don't want her in charge of anything to do with me anymore,' Chloe said vehemently.

He nodded. 'My lawyer will sort it out for you.'

Just like that! She shook her head in amazement, scarcely able to believe that the shackles of a lifetime could be broken so easily. 'My mother will fight against it. What did she say when you arranged this meeting?'

He shrugged. 'She wanted to speak to you, which I would not allow.'

'I don't want to listen to her.'

'I did pass that on,' he said dryly, totally unruffled by whatever arguments had been thrown at him.

Of course he wasn't emotionally involved, Chloe reasoned. To him it was a clear-cut business issue of ending an agent/actor contract and settling the financial fallout.

'Do I have to be at the meeting tomorrow?' she asked anxiously.

'Do you want to be?' He didn't seem to be the least bit concerned about it, again leaving the choice up to her.

'No.' She could well imagine the harangue she would be subjected to—the long list of all her mother had done for her. Except it wasn't for her. It had never been for her.

'Are you frightened your mother will persuade you to keep her on as your agent?' he asked curiously.

'No. I just don't want to listen to her. If you can work it without me...'

'It will undoubtedly go more smoothly without you. I'll have my lawyer join us for breakfast in the morning. You can give him your instructions and he'll act on them.'

'I think that would be best.'

Another decision made—by herself, for herself.

'Yes,' he agreed, rising from his chair. 'If you'll excuse me, Chloe, I'll call him now. Will eight o'clock suit?'

'Yes, but…' She looked down at her blue silk party dress. 'I have only these clothes.'

'A bathrobe will be fine for breakfast,' he assured her. 'I'll arrange for clothes to be brought to you from the hotel boutiques when they open. Don't worry about appearances. The big picture is more important.'

The big picture…one *she* was drawing, not her mother or Tony or even Maximilian Hart, who was giving her choices, not making decisions for her. She watched him move away, taking out his mobile phone to make the call to his lawyer. Somehow his power didn't feel quite so intimidating anymore. He was using it on her behalf—the white knight slaying her dragons.

She couldn't help liking him for it.

CHAPTER THREE

STEPHANIE ROLLINS did not bring a lawyer to the meeting. She walked into Max's office wearing power clothes—purple dress, wide red belt, red high heels, red fingernails—with the overweening confidence of a woman who had always held sway over her daughter and didn't believe that was about to change. Not even the presence of his lawyer shook her, not visibly. She viewed them both with a haughty disdain, as though Max was merely following through on his word, putting on a show.

The assumption was implicit that whatever Chloe had said to him last night, she would have backtracked on it this morning. There would be too big a void in her life without her mother. She wouldn't be able to cope on her own, had no-one else to turn to now that Tony Lipton had committed the unforgivable, destroying his credibility.

Max greeted her with cold courtesy, introduced her to Angus Hilliard, who headed his legal department, saw her seated and returned to his own chair behind the executive desk. 'As it turns out, there is no need for any discussion, Stephanie,' he said, gesturing for Angus to hand her the document severing her services as Chloe's agent.

She took it, read it, raised derisive eyes. 'This isn't worth the paper it's written on. Chloe will come back to me once she's calmed down. If you hadn't interfered last night, given your support…'

'Which she will continue to have.'

'Oh, I'm sure you'll look after what you perceive as *her* interests for the duration of her contract with you. It serves *your* interests. But after that…'

'I can steer Chloe to a reputable agent who will not take the exorbitant percentage of her earnings that you do,' Max slid in, his dislike of this woman so intense he intended to completely sabotage her influence over Chloe.

Anger spurted into her eyes. 'Without me she would be nothing. Chloe knows that. I engineered every step of her career, had her trained to be capable of carrying off any role, chose what would be the best showcase for her, pushed her into becoming the star you are now exploiting.'

'Yours is not the face that lights up the screen,' Max stated cuttingly. 'You didn't train you daughter to do that. It's a natural gift, which you have exploited for your own gain. In actual fact, you are nothing without her.'

Max enjoyed ramming that home, seeing the furious frustration in her eyes.

'You think you've got the upper hand?' she threw at him defiantly, rising to her feet and tossing the legal notice of separation on the desk. 'When your contract with Chloe is up, I'll see that she never signs another one with you.'

He eyeballed her with all the ruthless power at his command. 'Don't count on it, Stephanie. I'd advise you to use what you've milked out of your daughter to get a life of your own.'

She stared back, blazing fury gradually giving way to

speculative calculation. 'Why are you doing this? Why are you making it so personal?'

He shrugged and relaxed back in his chair, a sardonic smile playing on his lips. 'In this instance, the role of crusader for justice appeals to me.'

Her eyes narrowed. 'Or have you got the hots for Chloe? Seizing the moment?'

That shot was too close to the bone to ignore. He produced a mocking look. 'I am somewhat occupied with Shannah Lian, who, I doubt, would take kindly to that suggestion. Whatever my reputation with women, Stephanie, I'm not known for playing with two at the same time.'

'Whatever your interest is in Chloe, you'll move on. You always do,' she retorted, her chin lifting belligerently. 'And once you lose your interest in her, she'll come back to me.'

Never, Max thought with such violent feeling it surprised him. He watched Stephanie Rollins sail out of his office on her triumphant exit line, silently vowing she would not triumph. The door was slammed shut behind her to punctuate her power and Max instantly started planning to negate it.

'Phew! I'd hate to be in that woman's clutches,' Angus commented.

Max swivelled his chair to face the end of the desk where his lawyer was seated. Angus Hilliard was in his forties; bald, bespectacled and in the habit of hiding his incisive brain behind a mild manner. 'The trick is not to give those long red fingernails anything to draw blood from. She's had her pound of flesh, Angus.'

'That's for sure.' Behind the rimless glasses the lawyer's grey eyes glittered with the urge to act. 'From what Chloe told us over breakfast about everything she'd earned as a minor, I could probably get her mother for fraudulent appropriation of…'

'No. We don't dig up the past,' Max said firmly. 'Better for Chloe to close the door on that victimisation rather than relive it in court. I'm not sure she'd be up for it. Focusing on what she can do with the future is a far more positive step. And to give her the chance to take it, we have to stop her mother from getting to her.'

'Needs a bodyguard,' Angus suggested. 'Want me to arrange it?'

'Yes. Make it someone she'll feel comfortable with, a fatherly type, an experienced guy in his fifties. Have him come to my Vaucluse residence this afternoon for an interview with me.'

'Will do.' His mouth curved into a bemused little smile. 'I've never seen you as a crusader for justice, Max, but I have to admit…there's something about Chloe Rollins. Makes you want to do things for her.'

Her bodyguard would feel it, too, which was why Max didn't want some attractive young hunk tuning himself in to her needs. He needed time to re-organise his affairs, time for Chloe to like having him in her life, and he wasn't about to allow an attachment to develop with anyone else. He had to keep her on hold until he was ready to move.

'A rather special something,' he agreed, rising from his chair, smiling as he added, 'And it's no big deal for me to rescue and protect her. A small but satisfying challenge.'

Angus laughed. 'That's the Max I know. Very satisfying, winning against the monster mother. You're going back to the hotel now?'

'Yes. You'll tie up all the ends with Tony Lipton's contract?'

'With knots that can't be untied.'

Max nodded. 'Thanks for your help, Angus.'

He left, assured he hadn't shown his hand to anyone where Chloe Rollins was concerned. Nor would he until the time was right. A secret pleasure...the spice of anticipation...Max knew he would enjoy both as he waited.

Chloe could not relax. Her mind kept whirling around the idea of an independent life. It had shamed her this morning, revealing to Max and his lawyer how impossible it had been for her to strike out on her own. At eighteen, when she'd wanted to break free of her mother's demands on her, the money that was supposed to have been put in a trust account over the years of her childhood and adolescence was simply not there.

Her mother had been in control of all her earnings and had used them as she'd seen fit; buying a home for them, spending it on whatever she'd decided was right for Chloe's career, and right for her own as an agent to be reckoned with. With no funds and no training for anything else, her dream of independence had crumbled. She'd resigned herself to working as her mother directed, though insisting her financial share of any contract go straight into a bank account that only she could draw on.

She didn't actually dislike the work. Having constructed dream worlds for herself ever since she was a child, it was easy to slip into whatever role a director wanted her to play, but sometimes she yearned for a real life—one where there was no pretence involved, no putting on a show, no expectation of her beyond being herself.

Without her mother and Tony constantly pushing her into whatever limelight could be arranged, she could make her own choices, as she had been doing since Maximilian Hart had stepped in and given her that freedom. The thought of his meeting with her mother this morning made her shudder. Being there would have been awful. She was glad he had given her the option of letting him handle it. But learning how to handle things herself from now on was a necessary step to complete independence.

The telephone rang.

It had to be him.

The hotel people had been instructed not to put any other caller through to this suite.

She hurried to the writing desk and snatched up the receiver, her heart pounding with apprehension over what had occurred with her mother. 'Yes?' spilled anxiously from her lips.

'All done here,' came the calm reply. 'Your mother has been legally notified that she is no longer your agent. I'm on my way back to the hotel. Did you find something you liked amongst the selection of clothes sent up from the boutiques?'

So many questions were flooding her mind, it was difficult to focus on his enquiry. 'Oh…oh, yes I did, thank you. The salespeople took the rest back. I've jotted down the prices of what I chose to keep so I can repay you when I have access to my bank account.'

'No problem,' he said dismissively. 'I take it you're now happily dressed and ready to appear in public.'

Panic hit. 'How public?' Were there reporters ready to pounce outside the hotel, firing questions about Laura and Tony?

'Only lunch at the hotel, Chloe,' he assured her. 'I've booked a table for us at the Galaxy Restaurant. You'll be quite safe there in my company.'

Safe and hopefully more relaxed with him in a public restaurant, Chloe thought in relief. Alone with him in this private suite made her feel tense and nervous, too aware of her vulnerability to his powerful magnetism. 'Okay,' she said quickly. 'How did the meeting go?'

'We'll talk about it over lunch. Should be with you in half an hour. 'Bye now.'

Half an hour…

She put the receiver down and walked into the luxurious ensuite bathroom to check her appearance. The decor of this hotel—The Southern Cross—was all done in white, silver and shades of blue, which Chloe found very attractive. Blue was her favourite colour and she'd been instantly drawn to the blue-and-white polka dot dress, which she was now wearing.

It was a lovely soft silk in a wraparound style, with a wide white leather belt fastened with studs, which were covered by a large leather button. She'd chosen white toe-peeper high heels to go with it, and a plain white clutch bag, which was also fastened with a button. To her it was a smart, classy outfit that would come in handy for many occasions and was well suited for lunch in the premier restaurant of this hotel.

She'd carried a mini hairbrush and a few make-up essentials in her evening bag last night, so had been able to look reasonably presentable at breakfast this morning. She refreshed her lipstick, gave her hair a few flicks with the brush and decided no-one would find anything to criticise about her appearance. Especially not her mother, who wouldn't be there.

That thought lightened Chloe's spirits as she wandered back to the living area of the executive suite. This was a new day for her, and for the first time she noticed it was a beautiful day outside. The hotel was situated along the walkway to the Sydney Opera House and the floor-to-ceiling windows overlooked Circular Quay, as well as giving a magnificent view of the great coathanger harbour bridge. The sky was a cloudless blue, the water was sparkling and Chloe idly watched the ferries gliding into the quay and out again.

Her pulse rate instantly quickened when she heard the door to the suite being opened. There seemed to be nothing she could do to counter or defend against the strong impact of Maximilian Hart. He strode into the living area and stopped dead at seeing her standing in front of the long windows. The wild thought came to her that she had made some kind of surprising impact on him. Which was probably absurd, but for a few moments of stillness, there seemed to be an electricity in the air, zapping between them, vibrating along every nerve in her body.

'Mary...'

The name fell so softly from his lips, Chloe wondered if she'd heard correctly. 'I beg your pardon?'

He shook his head, a bemused little smile curving his mouth. 'You reminded me of someone.'

A woman he'd cared about? Chloe would have liked to ask about her, the momentary softness from him strongly piquing her curiosity, but almost instantly he shrugged it off and was the powerful man in charge again, walking purposefully towards her.

'Nice dress,' he said. 'It suits you.'

She flushed at the compliment though there was really nothing to it, only a bit of warm approval, and he didn't linger on it, moving straight to business as he handed her a sheet of paper.

'This needs your signature. It gives permission to the removalist company to enter your apartment at Randwick, pack up all your personal possessions and transport them to the guest house on my property at Vaucluse. I'll have it faxed to them once you've signed and they can get the job done this afternoon.'

It was all said in a matter-of-fact tone. Chloe took the sheet of paper, stared at it, tried to swallow the shock of the refuge he was offering. She wanted her things out of the apartment, needed a place to put them, but for it to be so closely connected to this man felt…dangerous. She hadn't thought ahead, didn't have an alternative plan to offer, yet….

'There must be apartments to let.' She raised anxious eyes to his. 'I don't feel comfortable about…'

'I can't guarantee your security anywhere else, Chloe.' The dark eyes mocked her fear of him. 'You won't be living with me. The guest house is quite separate to the main residence. The important issue is protection against any harassment, and not only from your mother or Tony. Once this scandal breaks, the media will go into a feeding frenzy, which means the paparazzi dogging your every move. You will be completely protected on my property. Consider it a pro tem arrangement, while you think about how best to handle your future.'

Yes, she did need time to make a proper plan—one she could and would stick to—and knowing all too well the tenacity of her mother, the point about protection against harassment was very appealing. Tony, too, might try to change her mind. Besides, how would she escape the inevitable outcome of all this with reporters chasing her and paparazzi shoving cameras in her face if she was trying to manage on her own? There was so much threatening her bid for freedom and Max was holding out safety from all of it.

She heaved a sigh to relieve the tightness in her chest. It didn't help. Another disturbing thought struck. 'There could be talk about us if I do this. I mean…with me leaving Tony…being with you…'

He looked sardonically amused by the intimation they could be lovers. 'I'll make it perfectly clear you're my guest, Chloe. I'm simply looking after the star of my show while she's dealing with a traumatic episode in her life.'

Heat surged into her cheeks again. It had been absurd of her to feel any danger in going with him. He wasn't about to use or abuse her. Besides, he was attached to another woman.

'Shannah Lian might not like it,' she blurted out.

He shrugged. 'I can take care of my own business, Chloe.'

Of course he could. Take care of hers, too. She felt foolish for even questioning the situation when he had already taken all aspects of it into account. 'Do you have a pen?' she asked, deciding her best course was to accept his offer.

He handed her one. She moved over to the coffee table, signed the permission note, then passed the pen and paper back to him with a smile of gratitude. 'It's very good of you to do all this for me.'

His smile smacked of deep, personal satisfaction. 'I'm a mover and shaker by nature. It pleases me to be of service to you.'

The white knight…except his eyes were dark and simmering with a pleasure that suddenly felt very sexual to Chloe. Her heart skipped a beat. Shockingly, her vaginal muscles clenched. It took an act of will to ignore this totally unwelcome physical arousal and divert her mind to something else.

'After you'd gone this morning I looked through the newspaper,' she babbled. 'I thought there might be some mention of the…the scandal. When you went back to the Starlight Room, didn't anyone say anything?'

'I made sure the story didn't break last night. I didn't think you were up to handling a hounding by the media and you're too exposed to it here in the hotel.'

Caring for her...

That was even more seductive than his physical magnetism. It was terribly difficult to keep any defences up against how he affected her.

'The story won't remain hidden,' he went on. 'Someone will talk. I simply bought enough time to set up a secure environment where no-one can gain access to you without your permission.'

She shook her head over how much care he had taken. It was extraordinary. But then *he* was extraordinary. The master player in action on her behalf.

'Thank you,' she said huskily, finding it difficult to even speak in a normal voice. She swallowed hard to work some moisture down her throat and ruefully added, 'Despite what you tell people, it will cause gossip, you know, with me leaving Tony and staying at your place.'

He looked at her consideringly. 'Will that worry you?'

She thought about it for several moments before answering, 'No. It will probably lessen the humiliation of the scandal, do my pride good being linked to you.' An ironic little smile accompanied the plain truth. 'You're a bigger fish than Tony.'

He laughed, his brilliant dark eyes lighting up with twinkles of amusement. 'Let me know if you get the urge to fry me.'

'Not much chance of that,' she swiftly retorted, heat racing into her cheeks again. 'You've never been caught.'

'Nor likely to be. I think most people would call me a shark.' He cocked a challenging eyebrow at her. 'You could try casting a net around me.'

It struck her that was precisely what *he* was doing, casting a net of security around her with ruthless efficiency. 'I don't have your power.'

'Not mine, but you do have power, Chloe,' he said on a more serious note. 'A different kind. It tugs at people. Even me.'

The self-mocking glint in his eyes told her that the white knight role was out of character for him. His true nature *was* that of a shark, always on the hunt, going after whatever attracted him, taking however many bites he wanted out of it, then cruising off, looking for other appealing prey to satisfy him. There wasn't a net that could hold this man. She'd always thought him intimidating, dangerous, powerful, and that impression was still very much in force.

However, it gave her a weird little thrill to know she tugged at something in him, too. Her mind shied away from the thought it was sexual. She was still married and he had Shannah Lian. It was probably more an arousal of sympathy that he didn't usually feel. Anyway, it made her feel less of an image he liked on the screen and more of a person he cared about.

'Well, whatever I have that tugs at you, I'm very grateful for it,' she said. 'You've provided me with an escape I couldn't have managed myself.'

'I hope it leads to a happier future.' He smiled, holding out his arm for her to take. 'Let's go and enjoy lunch.'

She grabbed her clutch bag from the coffee table and linked her arm to his, determined not to worry about his motives for helping her. 'What about the fax to the removalist company?' she reminded him, wanting her personal belongings out of the Randwick apartment and in her own possession as soon as possible.

'I'll hand it to the executive butler on this floor before we go down to the restaurant, instruct him to have it sent immediately.'

Chloe felt giddy with the thought that separation from her mother and Tony was being cemented in less than a day and she hadn't even had to face any fights over it. She hugged the arm of the man who had done this for her as they walked out of the hotel suite together, thinking how lucky she was to have a shark on her side, patrolling the waters around her, keeping bad things away.

Her whole body tingled at being in such close physical contact with him but it wasn't a tingle of fear or alarm, more one of excitement, pleasure in being attached to the power that had affected her freedom. She was acutely aware of the muscular strength of his arm, the whole male strength of him appealing to her female instincts, stirring a wish that he could always be at her side.

Which was totally unrealistic.

And weak, Chloe sternly told herself.

She had to learn to be strong on her own.

But right now, it felt amazingly good to be with Maximilian Hart.

CHAPTER FOUR

HILL House—a simple name for what was almost a historical mansion at Vaucluse. It had been built by Arthur Hill, an Australian shipping magnate who'd made a fortune early in the last century, and it had been lived in by his descendants until the last member of his family had died three years ago. There'd been a lot of publicity about it when it was put up for auction—photographs in magazines, a potted history of the Hill family, proceeds of the sale to go to various charities. Maximilian Hart had outbid everyone else for it.

At the time, it was generally assumed he'd bought it as another investment, which he'd sell when the market would give him a huge profit. After all, why would a jet-setting bachelor want to live in a mansion? Penthouse apartments would be more his style. Yet so far he had kept it and lived in it.

Maybe it was the privacy that appealed to him, Chloe thought, looking at the high brick wall enclosing the property as Max operated a remote control device that opened the huge iron gates facing them. They swung apart and he drove his black Audi coupe into the driveway to the house, pressing more buttons on the device to relock the gates.

While she had been quite relaxed over lunch in the hotel

restaurant, sitting beside him in his car on the way to an indefinite stay on his property had made her feel nervous again. So much proximity with Maximilian Hart was a rather daunting prospect. His kind and generous consideration of her needs could not be faulted, yet her instincts kept sensing an undertow that was pulling her into dangerous waters with him, especially when they were alone together.

The man was sexual dynamite. He stirred feelings and thoughts that were terribly inappropriate. As the gates clicked shut behind them, closing out the rest of Sydney—her mother, Tony and anyone else who might hassle her—Chloe could only hope the guest house Max had offered her was not somehow full of his powerful charisma…like his car.

The driveway was paved with grey stones. It bisected perfectly manicured green lawns. Some spectacular trees had been planted artistically along the wall and towards the side of the house—like a lovely frame for the house itself. There were no gardens to distract the eye from it.

The three-storey redbrick mansion was quite stunning in its beautiful symmetry. The wings at either end featured white gables. The main entrance in the middle also had a white gable held up by Doric columns. The long white many-paned windows on the second storey were perfectly aligned with the attic windows protruding from the grey roof. On the ground floor there were rows of matching glass doors that surely flooded the rooms behind them with sunlight.

Chloe instantly fell in love with Hill House. If she could have afforded to buy it she would have without hesitation. Envy and curiosity drove her to ask, 'Why did you buy this place, Max?'

He flicked her a sharp glance, making a swift assessment

of her reaction to the house, then smiled to himself as he answered, 'It called to me.'

His words surprised her, yet she completely understood the feeling behind them. 'You don't intend to sell it then?'

'Never.'

The need to know more about him prompted her to ask, 'Why does it call to you?'

'Everything about it pleases me. It welcomes me home every time I come through the gates.'

The deep satisfaction in his voice vibrated through her mind, stirring the memory of an article written about his rise from rags to riches. He'd been brought up by a single mother who'd died of a drug overdose when he was sixteen. Where he'd lived with her and under what conditions was not mentioned, but Chloe thought it likely he'd never had a sense of home in those early formative years.

'It's beautiful,' she murmured appreciatively. 'I can feel what you mean about welcoming. It makes you want to be drawn into it.'

'And stay there,' he said dryly. 'I virtually inherited the butler, the cook and the gardener from Miss Elizabeth, the last member of the Hill family. Although they had bequests from her will and could have retired on what they were given, they didn't want to leave. It was home to them, too.'

It was a curious arrangement for a man who undoubtedly made his own choices. 'Are you glad you kept them on?'

'Yes. They belong here. In a strange kind of way, they've become family. The three E's.' He flashed her a grin. 'Edgar is the butler. His wife, Elaine, is the cook. Eric is the head gardener. They have their own live-in apartments on the top floor. Eric hires help as he needs it and both Edgar and Elaine supervise the cleaners who come in. They run the place to such a standard of perfection I'd be a fool to hire anyone else.'

He parked the Audi in the wide stone-paved courtyard in front of the house, switched off the engine and turned to her. 'You'll be meeting Edgar in a moment. He likes to be very formal but you'll find him friendly. He'll show you to the guest house and give you a rundown on how everything works.'

It was a relief to know *he* would not be accompanying her there. She gave him a grateful smile. 'Thank you again for coming to my rescue.'

'No problem,' he answered dismissively.

Even as he escorted her to the gabled porch, the front door was opened by a tall, slightly portly man who held himself with straight-backed dignity. He was dressed in a black suit, grey-and-white striped shirt with white collar and cuffs and a grey silk tie. His hair was iron-grey, his eyes a light blue, his face surprisingly smooth for a man who looked to be about sixty. Possibly he didn't smile much, Chloe thought, preferring to carry an air of gravitas.

'Good afternoon, sir,' he intoned with a nod of respect.

'Edgar, this is Miss Chloe Rollins.'

She received a half-bow. 'A pleasure to welcome you to Hill House, Miss Rollins.'

'Thank you,' she replied, smiling warmly at him.

'I'll garage the car, then I'll be in the library, Edgar. Some business I have to do,' Max informed him. 'You'll take care of Miss Rollins?'

'Of course, sir.' He moved his arm in a slow gracious wave. 'If you'll accompany me, Miss Rollins, I'll escort you to the guest house.'

A wonderful butler, Chloe thought, as she fell into step

beside him, walking down a wide hallway dominated by a magnificent staircase that curved up to a balcony on the second floor—wonderful for making an entrance to greet incoming guests. The floor and stairs were carpeted in jade green bordered by a pattern of gold scrolls. The walls were panelled in western red cedar, matching the banister. The effect was very rich but not ostentatiously so.

There were paintings on the walls—framed in gold and seemingly all of birds—but Chloe didn't have time for more than a glance at them. They bypassed the staircase and she realised the hallway bisected the mansion and they were walking towards a set of double doors at the end of it, the upper half of them pannelled in a gloriously colourful pattern of parrots in stained glass. Other doors on either side of them were closed and Chloe would have loved to know what kind of rooms were behind them but didn't feel free to ask, given that she wasn't a guest in the mansion.

Edgar ushered her outside to a stunning terrace running the length of the house. The other three sides of it were semi-enclosed by an arched white pergola held up by the same Doric columns supporting the gable over the front doors. In the centre of the terrace was a sparkling swimming pool.

Luxurious green vines grew over the pergola providing shade for sun-loungers and tables and chairs made of white iron lace, and pots of flowers provided vivid colour at the foot of every column. The terrace itself was paved with slate, which had streaks of blue and green in what was mostly grey. Beyond it and through the open arches was a spectacular view of the harbour.

'The guest house is situated on the next terrace,' Edgar informed her, leading the way around the pool to the far left-hand corner of the pergola. 'It used to be the children's house in the old days.'

'The children's house?' Chloe quizzed. 'Didn't they live in the mansion?'

'Oh, yes, but they played down here during the day, supervised by their nanny. It was convenient for giving them lunch and snacks, putting the little ones down for afternoon naps. Miss Elizabeth said they loved having a place of their own. She kept it just the way it was until she died, often coming down here to relive memories of happy times.'

'Is it still the same?' She wanted it to be, charmed by the idea of a children's play house.

Edgar actually allowed himself a benevolent little smile at her eagerness. 'Not quite, no, though Mr Hart did retain the cottage style when he had it refurbished. The old pot-belly stove, the doll house, the bookshelves and the games cupboards still remain in the living room, with the addition of a television set and a DVD player. However, the kitchenette and bathroom had to be modernised. I'm sure you'll find it very comfortable, Miss Rollins.'

She sighed, wishing she could have seen it—felt it—in its original state, yet understanding the need for some modern conveniences in a guest house.

A flight of stone steps led down to the playground terrace—lush green lawn edged by a thickly grown hedge. The house was at one end of it—red brick with white windows and doors, just like the mansion in miniature. As they descended the steps, Chloe saw there was another terrace below this one, ending in a rock wall, which obviously formed a breakwater against encroachment from the harbour. A wharf ran out from it and beside the wharf was a boathouse.

Neither of these levels had been visible from the pool terrace. Access to them was by flights of steps, as well as a rather steep driveway from top to bottom just inside the security wall on the left-hand side, mainly used, Chloe imagined, by Eric driving a mini-tractor carrying garden tools up and down.

Edgar unlocked the door to the guest house, handed her the key and with a rather grandiloquent gesture, waved her in. Chloe walked into a delightfully cosy living area, which ran the full width of the small house. To her left were two rockers and a sofa upholstered in rose-patterned chintz. A large bow window had a cushioned window seat where one could curl up and read or idly watch the traffic on the harbour. A thick cream mat covered the parquet floor in front of the pot-belly stove, perfect for lying on near the heat in winter. An entrancing doll house stood in one corner near the bow window, a television set in the other. Cupboards lined the bottom half of the wall next to the front door, bookshelves the upper half.

To her right was a country-style round table with six chairs, and behind it a kitchenette, also designed in a country style— varnished wood cupboards and a white sink, no stainless steel visible anywhere. Edgar showed her the pantry cupboard, saying, ' My wife, Elaine, has stocked it with the usual staples, but if there's something else you'd particularly like, just press the kitchen button on the telephone and ask her for it.'

He also opened the refrigerator, which was similarly stocked with staples plus a chicken casserole ready to slide into the oven for her dinner tonight. 'Please thank Elaine for me,' Chloe said gratefully. 'This is so good of her.'

Another small benevolent smile. 'Let me show you the rest of the house.'

There were two bedrooms and a bathroom in between. The old bath, Edgar told her, had been replaced by a shower stall to leave room enough for the addition of the washing machine and clothes dryer. What had once been designated the boys' room held two single beds. The girls' room held one—queen-size. All of them had beautiful patchwork quilts. Both rooms had wall-length storage cupboards, plenty of room to hold all her personal things, although Chloe didn't intend to unpack everything, just enough for her immediate needs.

Edgar checked his watch. 'It's just on a quarter past three o'clock now. The removalist company gave their estimated arrival time here at four-thirty. Eric, Mr Hart's gardener and handyman, will conduct the transport of boxes to you, Miss Rollins, help you open them and remove those you wish to unpack after they've been emptied. Others can remain stored in the boys' room. In the meantime, if there's anything else...?'

'No, thank you, Edgar. I'll enjoy myself exploring everything I have here.'

'You're very welcome, Miss Rollins,' he said and bowed himself out of the house.

Chloe made herself a cup of coffee, sipping it as she checked out the contents of the bookshelves. There was a stack of CDs providing a range of classical and popular music, several shelves of modern books—most she recognised as bestsellers in both fiction and non-fiction. However, her interest was mainly drawn by the old books; Dickens, Robert Louis Stevenson, Edgar Allan Poe, the whole series of *Anne of Green Gables* and *Pollyanna*, an ancient set of Encyclopedia Britannica, a book containing drawings of birds—not photographs—a history of ships, a guide for all sorts of fancy needlework.

Her imagination conjured up the nanny teaching the girls how to sew, the boys identifying birds from the book, scenes of a happy childhood she had never known but which leapt vividly into her mind. She felt a strong wave of empathy with Miss Elizabeth, sitting in this room, opening these books to leaf through them again, reliving her memories.

The cupboards held more old treasures; a slightly tattered but still intact game of Monopoly, boards for snakes and ladders with coloured discs and dice for playing and Chinese checkers with sets of pegs, a chess set made of marble, packs of cards, boxes of jigsaws from very simple to very challenging. Chloe decided to start one of them tonight. It would be much more fun than watching television.

She finished her coffee and moved on to the most entrancing piece from the past—the doll house. It was made of wood and was double-storeyed. Its roof was hinged so it could be lifted up to rearrange the rooms on the second floor—the bedrooms amazingly well-furnished, cupboards, chairs, dressing-tables with mirrors, even little patchwork quilts on the beds. The bathroom had a miniature china tub with iron claw feet, a washstand, a tiny china toilet.

All the windows and doors could be opened and shut. The ground floor was just as amazing. A central hallway held a staircase to the upper floor. A fully fitted-out dining room and kitchen were situated on one side of it, on the other an exquisitely furnished sitting room and behind it a utility room with laundry tubs.

Chloe was sitting on the floor, one finger stroking the silk brocade on a miniature sofa, when a loud tapping startled her out of her enthralment with the little masterpiece. Her head jerked around. Her heart kicked as her gaze met the dark brilliant eyes of Maximilian Hart looking straight at her through the multi-paned glass door. A hot flush zoomed into her cheeks as she scrambled to her feet, feeling hopelessly disarmed at being caught out doing something so childish.

She worked hard at regathering her composure as she crossed the living room and managed a rueful little smile when she opened the door. 'I didn't have a doll's house when I was a little girl,' she said, shrugging away her absorption in it.

'Were you ever allowed to be a little girl, Chloe?' he asked with a flash of sympathy.

She grimaced. 'It wasn't an ordinary life. My mother…' Her voice trailed off, her mind instinctively shutting out thoughts of her mother.

'Mine wasn't ordinary, either,' he said with a touch of black irony, then with a quizzical look, asked, 'Do you have the sense of something very different in this children's house?'

'Yes. Yes, I do,' she answered eagerly. 'I love the feel of it, Max.'

He nodded, and there was something in his eyes—a recognition of all she had missed out on, perhaps an echo of his own lost boyhood. It tugged at her heart, making it flip into a faster beat. Then it was gone, replaced by an intensity of purpose, which left her floundering in an emotional morass.

'May I come in?'

Embarrassment increased the floundering. She'd left him standing on the doorstep instead of inviting him in. 'Of course. Please…' She quickly stepped back, giving him plenty of room to enter, every nerve in her body quivering from the magnetic force field he brought with him.

'Leave the door open,' he instructed. 'I just wanted a private word with you before introducing the bodyguard who's waiting outside.'

'Bodyguard!' Shock galvanised her attention.

'I've employed him to drive you to and fro from the set at Fox Studios, or anywhere else you wish to go. He'll stay close to you while ever you're away from this property, ensure you're not harassed by anyone. It's simply a safeguard, Chloe, nothing for you to worry about. You can dispense with his services later on, but I think to begin with, you'll feel more secure having him around.' He made an apologetic grimace. 'Unfortunately, I have other calls on my time and can't always be on hand to protect you.'

'No. I wouldn't expect it of you,' she swiftly assured him, acutely conscious of the time he'd already spent on her.

'I'd like you to accept the bodyguard, if only to make me feel I've covered every contingency for avoiding problems you might be faced with. I do hate failure,' he said in a self-mocking tone.

Considering all he had done for her, Chloe felt it was impossible not to oblige him on this point, though she thought a bodyguard was excessive. 'All right. If you really think it's necessary,' she said uncertainly.

'I do.'

No uncertainty in his mind. He immediately walked back outside and beckoned to someone who must have been waiting at the foot of the stone steps. Chloe imagined some big, burly hunk of a man, like a bouncer at a nightclub. It was a relief to see almost a fatherly figure, conservatively dressed in a grey suit, his salt-and-pepper hair and the lines of experience on his face suggesting he was in his fifties. He was as tall as Max, broad-shouldered, barrel-chested, and Chloe had no doubt he had a strong enough physique to impose his will on others, but he didn't look like a bully-boy, more a mature man who wore a confident air of authority and the muscle to impose it if needed.

Max performed the introductions. 'Miss Chloe Rollins, Gerry Anderson.'

A strong hand briefly pressed the one she offered. 'At your service, Miss Rollins. I'm Gerry to everyone so please feel free to use the name,' he invited in a deep, pleasant voice.

'Thank you. I hope I'm no real trouble to you,' she said sincerely.

'I'll be taking care of any that comes your way, Miss Rollins,' he assured her, taking a slim mobile telephone from his coat pocket. 'I'll be here six o'clock Monday morning to take you to work. If you want to go out anywhere before then, contact me with this and we'll make arrangements.' He showed her his stored contact number, then gave her the phone, satisfied she knew how to work it.

It was Saturday afternoon. She would probably be busy unpacking most of Sunday and there was plenty of food here to keep her going. 'Thank you, but I won't be going anywhere tomorrow,' she said decisively.

'Keep it with you. I'm on call anytime, day and night.'

'Okay,' she agreed.

'Thank you, Gerry,' Max said in dismissal.

The older man raised a hand in salute to both of them and made a prompt exit, leaving Chloe alone with Max again. The dark eyes bored into hers, as though tunnelling a path to her heart, which instantly started a nervous pounding.

'Since you have a good feeling in this house, Chloe, I suggest you stay here until the current twelve episodes of the show have been completed. It will be easier for you, no disruptive tensions to interfere with your work, and I can house any guests I wish to invite in the mansion, so it will not present any problem to me.'

Two months living here…it was so seductive.

But two months in close proximity to him…

'Think about it,' he commanded in a soft, persuasive tone. 'I just want you to know you're welcome to stay.'

'Thank you,' she managed to say, hoping he couldn't see her inner turmoil.

'And please feel free to use the swimming pool at any time,' he went on with a smile that put flutters in her stomach. 'They've forecast a very hot day tomorrow.'

'Thank you,' she said again, and wondered if she sounded like a parrot mimicking words that really meant nothing.

'Relax, Chloe.' His eyes turned to a soothing chocolate velvet and he reached out and gently stroked her cheek. 'Be happy here.'

It was the lightest feather touch, yet it left a hot tingling that Chloe felt for several minutes after he was gone. She didn't accompany him to the door. He walked out himself while she stood in a mesmerised trance, her own hand automatically lifting to cover the highly sensitised cheek, whether to hold on to the feeling or make it go away, she didn't know.

What she did know with utter certainty was that Maximilian Hart affected her as no other man had…deeply…and while it frightened her, it also excited her, as though he was opening doors she wanted to go through…with him.

CHAPTER FIVE

MAX occupied one of the sun-loungers under the eastern pergola, idly doing the Sudoku puzzles from one of the Sunday newspapers. From time to time he glanced to the far northern corner of the terrace, expecting Chloe to appear at the top of the flight of steps, coming to the pool for a swim. It was a hot morning, so hot that a storm would probably brew up this afternoon. The shade of the vines and the light breeze from the harbour made his waiting tolerable.

He'd done all the groundwork to achieve what he wanted. He was sure Chloe would accept his invitation to stay, just as he was sure of the sexual chemistry at work between them. Restraint had to be kept for a while. A delicate hand had to be played, no pushing too hard, too soon. Any sense of being dominated by him had to be avoided.

She'd had that with her mother and having made the break from Stephanie's overbearing control, she would shy from falling into a similar situation. He had to make her feel whatever she did from now on was her own choice, but he'd be leading her to wanting him every step of the way—wanting him as much as he wanted her.

The strength of his desire surprised him. It wasn't his usual style to get so involved with a woman. All his relationships in the past had revolved around having regular sex with women he liked—an urge he took pleasure in satisfying. He could have had it last night with Shannah. She'd invited him to even after he'd told her their affair was over—a final farewell in bed—yet he'd been totally disinterested in anything physical with her. She'd accepted his dry, goodbye kiss on the cheek with wry grace—still friends, despite his moving on.

Chloe had been on his mind. It had been difficult to even focus his attention on Shannah. Thoughts of what Chloe might be doing in the children's house kept intruding, plans for how best to draw *her* into sharing his bed.

Her husband was history but Max didn't feel right about storming her into an affair with him. She was too vulnerable right now. It would be like taking advantage of a wounded creature. He had to wait, but the mental force to keep his desire in check needed considerable bolstering when he looked up and saw her moving towards the pool.

She wore a simple turquoise maillot, cut high on the leg and with a low enough V-neckline to reveal the swell of her breasts. Every lovely feminine curve of her body was on display and he instantly felt a tightening in his groin. It took an act of will to relax again and simply watch her.

She was unaware of his presence. The glare of bright sunlight made him virtually invisible in the shade of the pergola. She dropped the towel she'd been carrying by the edge of the pool, removed her sandals and waded in via the steps, which ran its width at the shallow end. The water was solar-heated to a temperature that kept it refreshing without being chilly. She smiled her pleasure as she slowly lowered herself into it and made soft waves with her arms. Max found the dimples in her cheeks strangely endearing, childlike, and he smiled himself, feeling a wave of indulgence towards her.

She didn't break into a swim. She pushed off from the steps and glided, rolling her body over and over, wallowing in the water, floating, her wet hair drifting around her like a golden halo. He could have remained watching her for much longer, enjoying her uninhibited pleasure, but when she started swimming, splashing, the noise made his own silence questionable. He rose from the lounger and moved to his end of the pool ready to greet her when she reached it.

'Good morning.'

Chloe was so startled by the greeting, she almost lost her grip on the ledge, which formed a seat at the deep end. Her head jerked up. She'd thought there was no-one on the terrace, that she had the pool to herself, but it was Max's voice. Max was here. He stood barely a metre away, and her heart started hammering as her stunned mind registered the fantastic body of the man—naked but for a brief black swimming costume that left very little to the imagination.

He had the physique of an Olympic swimmer, broad shoulders and chest, strong arms, every male muscle impressively delineated, lean waist and hips, powerful thighs and calves, and his tanned skin gleamed as though it was polished. It was all so in her face, she couldn't find the breath to speak.

He smiled apologetically. 'Sorry to startle you. I was reading the newspapers under the pergola.' He waved to where he'd been sitting. 'When I heard you swimming, I thought I'd refresh myself, as well. Mind if I join you?'

'No. No, of course not,' she gabbled. It was his pool.

'Did you sleep well?'

'Yes. Like a baby.' She grimaced at the phrase, reminded of the baby Laura would have, the baby she had been denied.

He saw the grimace and frowned. 'Everything all right for you in the guest house?'

'Perfect,' she assured him, smiling to wipe out his concern.

'Good!' He grinned. 'Let's swim.'

He dived into the pool, barely making a splash and broke surface almost halfway down it, moving straight into a classic crawl. Chloe hitched herself onto the underwater seat and watched him as he swam the length and back again, using the few minutes trying to stop her heart from racing and her mind from dwelling on the fact that Maximilian Hart left every other man for dead when it came to physical attraction.

Tony's physique was well-proportioned but it didn't have that much male power. Amazingly, her mind hadn't been churning over Tony and Laura since she'd been here. It was as though they had drifted off to a far distance and she was already immersed in an existence without them. Was it because Max put himself between her and them, blotting them out with his overwhelming presence, or was it the effect of the children's house, giving her such pleasant distraction?

Both had played their part.

She was safe from the others if she stayed here, safe from horrible, hurtful arguments with Tony, safe from the pressure her mother would apply with every bit of emotional blackmail she could concoct.

But was she safe with a shark?

The thought popped into her mind as Max finished cutting through the water and hauled himself onto the seat beside her, his dark brilliant eyes teasing as he asked, 'Did I scare you off swimming?'

She laughed to hide the tension triggered by his nearness. 'No way could I keep up with you.'

'I'll go slow,' he promised.

'A very leisurely pace.'

'You've got it.'

She plunged into the water ahead of him, wanting the activity to calm her down, soothe her twitching nerve ends. Max wasn't coming onto her. He was just being himself. Besides, he had Shannah Lian. Of course she was safe with him.

They swam several lengths of the pool together. It was impossible not to be acutely aware of the man beside her, but Chloe managed to put the situation in enough perspective to feel reasonably comfortable with his company when she called a halt at the shallow end where she'd left her towel.

'Enough?' he asked.

'For now,' she answered, walking up the steps, so conscious of her own body under his gaze, she quickly snatched up her towel and wrapped it around her.

'I hate to put a dampener on the day, but I think you should see what Lisa Cox has written in the entertainment section of her Sunday newspaper,' he said as he followed her out of the pool.

She swung around in dismay. 'Is it bad?'

'Somewhat sensational,' he answered sardonically, waving towards the eastern pergola. 'Come and read it for yourself. I'll pour you a cool drink that might make it more palatable.'

She fell into step with him as he headed back to where he'd sat, anxiety and apprehension overriding most of her awareness of his almost naked state. Nevertheless, when they reached the welcome shade of the pergola, she was relieved that he picked up a towel from one of the loungers and tucked it around his waist.

The newspapers were on a nearby table, which also held a tray with some long glasses and a cooler bag, obviously containing a pitcher of whatever liquid Max was going to serve her. He moved to the table, drew out one of the chairs for her, then tapped the top newspaper as he reached for the cooler bag.

'This one. Take a seat, Chloe.' He busied himself opening the bag and removing a large jug of fruit juice while he talked. 'Apparently Tony broke the story. Out of spite, I should think, after the removalists had left to transport your personal possessions here. He'd demanded what authority they had and they'd shown him the fax, giving this address.'

Maximilian Hart's mansion at Vaucluse…it was a big step up from the apartment at Randwick, while Tony was out in the cold, fired from the script-writing team, and powerless to stop what was happening. Chloe could see him wanting to do something spiteful, yet how could he exonerate his own behaviour?

'Lisa Cox telephoned me late yesterday afternoon to get confirmation of your presence on my property and my comment on it,' Max went on. 'She wanted to speak to you, as well, but I'd left you reasonably happy in the children's house and didn't think you'd want to be stirred up by nasty innuendos, so I told her you were unavailable.'

He poured the juice into two glasses and sat one in front of her, a flash of inquisitive appeal in his eyes. 'I hope you don't mind my running interference for you with Lisa.'

She shook her head. 'I'm sure you handled the situation better than I would have.'

He shrugged and took the chair opposite hers, the expression in his eyes changing to a hard, ruthless gleam as he flatly stated, 'I told her the truth.' His mouth twisted cynically and his voice took on a mocking tone. 'Tony had reported that you'd left him for me, omitting the salient facts like his infidelity and impregnating your personal assistant. I laid them out and apparently your mother has confirmed them, while hitting out at me for taking you away when you should be with her, being comforted as only a mother can comfort in such stressful circumstances. She made no mention of having her services as your agent terminated.'

Chloe grimaced at his summary of Tony's and her mother's spin on what had happened. 'I'm sorry, Max. I did warn you there'd be a backlash to protecting me as you have.'

'Makes me more determined to keep doing so.' His eyes flashed intensity of purpose at her. 'You need a complete break from them, Chloe. Best that you stay here the two months, avoid all aggravation. As I said, it's no problem for me if you do, and it will hold you clear of them so you can work out your own future.'

He liked being in charge of a battle zone, Chloe thought. A born warrior. And she liked being protected by him. Probably too much. But she could learn how best to stand up for herself from him.

'I'd better read the whole thing,' she muttered, opening up the newspaper and lifting out the entertainment section.

The story was headlined Maximilian Hart's Star Hit by Scandal. It held much more detail than Max had given; rantings from Tony about Max taking her over, using his power to alienate her from their marriage; her mother taking a similar stance, saying Max had inserted himself between mother and daughter with no regard for what was appropriate or what was in Chloe's best interests. They more or less painted him as a ruthless manipulator, which wasn't the truth at all.

Max had stated the truth—that she'd been deeply shocked

and distressed by the disclosure at the launch party that her husband had been having an affair with her trusted personal assistant who was now pregnant to him, and she hadn't wanted to go home to either her husband or her mother, so he'd offered her his guest house as a ready refuge where she was welcome to stay as long as she liked. The story ended, saying Chloe Rollins had not been available for comment.

'You could sue them for slander over the things they've said about you,' she murmured fretfully.

'Irrelevant,' he said carelessly, then shot her an ironic smile. 'Much better not to give them a stage to star on. Let them fade into insignificance as the show moves on.'

Chloe returned some irony of her own. 'You know what the most sickening part is? Both my mother and Tony talked me out of having a baby because starring in your show was more important.'

His gaze dropped from hers as he frowned over this new information.

'I guess you wouldn't have wanted me if I had been pregnant,' she put to him, interpreting his frown as confirmation that her mother and Tony had been right about that.

He shook his head. 'Nothing would have changed my determination to star you in that particular vehicle.' His eyes targeted hers again with their riveting power. 'If you had been pregnant, Chloe, I would have had the storyline altered to accommodate it.'

'Really?'

His mouth twitched with amusement at her wide-eyed wonderment. 'Really.'

'Then they were wrong.' It was weird how much satisfaction that gave her, as though it totally vindicated her current course of action. 'Not that it matters,' she added. 'It would be a worse mess now if I had got pregnant, with Tony fooling around with Laura behind my back. And I bet my mother knew about it, too. Nothing escapes her eye.'

'I'd say that was a fair assumption,' Max dryly commented. 'She showed no outrage or disgust over their behaviour when I confronted them at the hotel. Only anger over the boat being rocked.'

Anger... Chloe winced, having been belittled by it too many times. And she'd always hated the strident way her mother dealt with other people, even with the man sitting opposite her, making sure she saw and covered all the angles. It was an agent's job, but the manner in which it was done... Chloe imagined Max had quite enjoyed severing the business connection with her mother. It was a huge relief to feel free of it herself.

She sipped her drink, noticing that Max seemed to have drifted into a private reverie, gazing out across the pool, his eyes narrowed as though he was thinking through a problem, assessing its effects, how to deal with it. After a few minutes, he turned to her with a curious, inquisitive look.

'Tell me...you're only twenty-seven, Chloe...are you desperate for a baby?'

She flushed, embarrassed at having babbled on about having one, knowing many women waited until their early thirties before starting a family. 'Not desperate, no,' she quickly denied, then with a rueful little shrug, confessed, 'I just wanted to have something I knew was real in my life. My mother would twist things around. Tony did, too. But a baby...well, there's nothing more honest about a baby, is there?'

'Honest,' he repeated musingly.

'I'm glad it didn't happen,' she blurted out. 'It would have chained me to Tony for the rest of my life.'

'Yes. At least this way you can put him behind you.'

She grimaced. 'Except for the divorce.'

'That can all be done through lawyers,' he said dismissively. 'There's no need for you to meet. I was just wondering if you had the urge to rush into bed with someone else and get yourself pregnant.'

It shocked her into a vehement denial. 'I'm not that stupid, Max!'

He shook his head. 'I don't think you're stupid, Chloe, but people often don't react sensibly to a traumatic change in their lives.'

'I have a big enough problem sorting out my own life,' she insisted. 'I wouldn't add a baby to it.'

He smiled, satisfied that she was not about to run madly off the rails and ruin this chance to get herself straight on a lot of things. Yet she sensed something more in his satisfaction—something sharkish. A little quiver ran down her spine.

'I'm hungry,' he said. 'It's lunch-time.'

Chloe breathed a sigh of relief. The something sharkish had nothing to do with wanting a bite out of her.

He picked up a mobile phone, which had lain behind the tray. 'I'll call Edgar to bring it out here. Shall I say lunch for two? It won't be any trouble to Elaine. I ordered salad and she always keeps enough provisions for an army.'

The invitation was irresistible. Despite the occasionally disturbing undercurrent of strong physical attraction she couldn't quite ignore, she liked talking to him, liked hearing his view of her situation, liked the way it clarified things in her own mind. She didn't want to end this encounter by the pool. Besides, having eaten the scrumptious chicken casserole last night, the offer of another meal prepared by Elaine was an extra temptation.

'Thank you. I'd like that.'

Max watched her smile, the sweet curve of her lips, the dimples appearing in her cheeks, the warm pleasure sparkling in her lovely blue eyes, and thought how artlessly beautiful she was. She wore no make-up. Her hair was drying in natural waves around her face—tighter than if she'd used a blow dryer. Her skin glowed, not a blemish on it anywhere.

He wanted to touch her, taste her, but now was not the time. He called Edgar and ordered lunch for two by the pool, knowing he had to keep this encounter a casual one, relaxing, enjoyable, trouble-free, building the case for her to stay the two months.

The baby issue had been a snag in his plans. It was a relief to have it dismissed. Though, for a few moments, that something special about Chloe had actually had him wondering how life would be if they filled the children's house together. A brief flight of fancy. Not really feasible, given the jet-setting life he enjoyed, winning the challenges that added to his success in the battlefield he'd chosen.

They spent another two hours by the pool, sharing a leisurely lunch, chatting about the television business. He kept the conversation impersonal—safe—drawing Chloe out on how she saw and felt about the show, her part in it, her view of the other cast members and how they were dealing with their roles.

'You know, Max, I don't have a special gift for tapping into emotion on cue,' she said at one point. 'It's not like some magic I was born with. When I get a part to play, I make up the whole life behind the character so I know everything about her in my mind, why she is doing or feeling the way she does in various situations. When I'm on camera, I am her. It's real. I show it. That's all.'

He respected the work she put into adopting a character, but she was wrong about not having a special gift. It was innate. The play of emotion was on her face all the time in her own life. He didn't have to study her to read her feelings. They were mirrored in her expressions.

He'd first noticed her in a coming-of-age soap opera that had run for years. She outshone everyone else in the cast. He'd learnt that she'd been on television all her life—commercials featuring a baby, then a toddler, children's shows, teenage shows. He kept her in mind, waiting to acquire a storyline that would showcase her special talent, and she certainly wasn't disappointing him now that he had it.

By all accounts, her father had also been a very gifted actor. There were still people around who deplored his early death—suicide, in the grip of depression. He couldn't imagine Stephanie doing anything to help him out of it, more like driving him into it with her self-serving demands.

He didn't want Chloe falling into a depression, unable to put it aside to play her part in the show—a very solid reason for her to be here with him, out of her mother's reach. She looked happy at the moment. Nevertheless, he couldn't control her mood when she was alone.

An idea came to him. She'd wanted a baby. He'd give her a puppy or a kitten, something for her to look after and pet, another attraction for staying in the children's house and it should lessen any loneliness she felt.

As it turned out, he didn't need to add another attraction.

Edgar had been and gone with his tray-mobile, clearing the table and leaving them with coffee and a selection of Elaine's petit fours. It more or less marked the end of lunch and Max knew he shouldn't press Chloe into staying longer with him if she made a move to go. She finished her coffee and faced him with an air of decision.

'I will stay the two months, Max.'

She said a lot more, expressing her gratitude for his offer, etc, etc, but he barely heard it, his mind buzzing with elation.

He'd won.

And he'd win all he wanted with Chloe Rollins before she left the children's house.

She was his for the taking.

CHAPTER SIX

CHLOE was glad she had accepted Gerry Anderson's services on Monday morning, glad that Max had instructed him to use the black Audi Quattro sedan with tinted windows for transporting her wherever she wanted to go. Paparazzi were camped outside the gates of the Vaucluse mansion. They were also at the entrance to the studios. Interest in the scandal was obviously running hot.

Once they were safely inside the grounds of the studio, she asked Gerry to stop the car and summon the security guard so she could speak to him. She rolled down her window as the man approached.

'Miss Rollins?' He tipped his cap to her.

She smiled. 'Good morning. I just wanted you to know that my mother, Stephanie Rollins, is no longer my agent and I would not welcome her on the set.'

He nodded. 'Mr Hart has already given instructions to that effect. Covers Mr Lipton and Miss Farrell, as well. Don't be worrying they'll be let in, Miss Rollins. They won't.'

'Thank you.'

'No problem,' he assured her with a friendly salute.

Max…one step ahead of her. He thought of everything. But

at least she had acted decisively for herself this time and Chloe felt good about that. She was never going to allow anyone to make decisions for her again, or be talked into anything she didn't want to do.

The whole day on the set felt better without her mother sitting in on everything, watching, criticising, coaching, fussing. No-one there was unaware of her situation, and at first the other cast members and the crew treated her with a kind of wary sympathy. Only after she had demonstrated that she was still on top of her role and determined to carry through every scene to be shot did they become more relaxed with her. Chloe felt her own confidence growing as she followed the director's instructions without a hitch.

Sympathy gave way to curiosity. She wasn't acting like a traumatised woman. Had she left her unfaithful husband and plunged into an affair with Maximilian Hart? No-one put it into words but Chloe read the speculation in their eyes. Oddly enough, she wasn't embarrassed by it. While it wasn't the truth, she sensed that people wouldn't blame her for it if she had. In fact, during the break for lunch, there was envy in some of the women's eyes when one guy brashly asked her if Max's guest house matched his mansion.

'It's much smaller,' she answered dryly, and her quelling look put an immediate stop to any further questions touching on her private life. She didn't want to describe how special the children's house was, nor reveal her decision to stay on there for two months. It was no-one else's business but hers and Max's.

However, she inadvertently broke the confidentiality of their arrangement later that afternoon. After leaving the studios, she asked Gerry to drive her to her favourite green-grocer's market at Kensington, wanting to stock up with fruit and vegetables and be relatively independent of Elaine's provisions for the guest house. Gerry insisted on accompanying her into the market, saying the car had been followed, although not into the parking station, which allowed some room for doubt as to whether the pursuit had been coincidental or deliberate.

Coincidental, Chloe thought. The tinted windows of the car had frustrated the paparazzi this morning. Why waste their time following her again? Max was the better target and she wasn't with him.

But it was deliberate.

Chloe had only been shopping for a few minutes when an all too familiar voice cracked at her like a whip with stinging force.

'It's a shameful state of affairs when a mother is reduced to chasing a car to make contact with her daughter!'

The lettuce she'd been holding spilled from her hand. Her heart jumped and so did the rest of her body as she spun to face the oncoming attack. Her mother was livid with anger, her steel-blue eyes shooting furious arrows of accusation, her hands already lifting like talons to grab Chloe's shoulders and shake her. The old instinct to cringe swept through her but this time Chloe fought it. She was not a child to be shaken into submission and her mother did not *own* her anymore. Her spine stiffened and she stood her ground, although her stomach cramped and her legs started to tremble.

Gerry Anderson stepped between them and her chest almost caved in with relief at being shielded by him.

'Get out of the way! She's my daughter!' her mother hissed, grabbing his arm, trying to pull him aside.

'Miss Rollins?' Gerry was looking to her for direction.

He would strong-arm her mother away and swiftly escort

her out of here if she gave the word. The temptation to flee quivered through her mind, but she'd been weak for far too long, letting her mother run her life. Running away from her now meant she still had power over her, would always have power over her. It had to stop if she was ever to forge an independent life.

She shook her head. 'I'll talk to her but stay near, Gerry.' She turned to her mother, eyes flashing determination. 'If you create any more of a scene, my bodyguard will step in and we'll go. Is that clear, Mother?'

'*Your* bodyguard,' she savagely mocked as Gerry stepped aside for the two women to face each other. 'Max Hart's, you mean. He's taking you over, lock, stock and barrel and you're too blindly naive to see it.'

'He is simply protecting me from the kind of harassment you're dealing out right now.'

'And why is he doing it, Chloe? Have you asked yourself that?'

'I don't care why. I'm out of the mess of my marriage, which you hid from me so I'd keep on working and bringing in the money. I'm not so blindly naive that I can't see that, Mother.'

'You've been working today to bring in the money for Max Hart.'

'*He* didn't deceive me.'

'It was for your own good,' she snapped defensively. 'The affair would have blown over without any pain for you if Laura hadn't got herself pregnant.'

'I don't like your judgement of what is good for me. I'm not going to take it anymore.'

'You need me, Chloe,' she bored in. 'You'll be lost without me. I've handled everything for you for so long…'

'I'll learn to do it myself.'

'You think that can be done in a day?' she jeered.

'No. I expect it will take a while.'

'Making a host of *bad* judgements. For a start, where do you intend to live?'

Chloe hesitated, not having thought that far yet.

'You can't stay in Max's guest house forever,' her mother pushed, mocking Chloe's indecision.

'No, of course not.'

Maybe her lack of any urgent concern over where to live gave the situation away.

Her mother pounced. 'He's invited you to stay on, hasn't he? How long?'

'This is none of your business!' Chloe retorted defensively.

'Longer than a few days. Longer than a week for you to think you don't need me. A month? Two months?' Speculation turned to triumphant certainty. 'Yes. Two months. Until shooting all the episodes for the show is over. That would suit him very nicely. And you're so gullible you got sucked right in.'

'It suits me, too,' Chloe hotly insisted, hating how her mother twisted everything.

Her claim was dismissed with a derisive snort. 'Out of the frying pan into the fire!'

'What's that supposed to mean?'

Her eyes glittered with contempt for Chloe's intelligence. 'Max Hart is worse than Tony, flitting from woman to woman. He's setting you up for when he gets rid of Shannah Lian. Which will be very soon. Mark my words! You won't have two months free of him. I'll bet the bank on that.'

Dangerous…the undertow of physical attraction…impossible to ignore yet she hated her mother's interpretation of the situation.

'You'll end up in a bigger mess than you have now,' she went on in her disparaging voice. 'You need me, Chloe. *I'm* the one who's always protected you. Max Hart is a shark. He'll eat you up and when you've satisfied his sexual appetite…'

'That's enough!' Chloe cried. 'I don't have to listen to this and I won't! Gerry…' She turned to him in urgent appeal. 'I want to go now.'

He immediately hooked one arm around hers, holding the other one out in a warding-off gesture. 'Excuse us, Mrs Rollins,' he said politely, starting to move Chloe along the shopping aisle towards the exit.

'When you know I'm right, come home to me,' her mother sliced at her. 'I'll look after you.'

Chloe maintained a stony face, looking straight ahead, refusing to acknowledge the claim that she couldn't look after herself.

She would.

As for the rest, Max wouldn't force her into anything she didn't want.

All along he had given her choices.

Not like her mother, who dictated what was to be done.

And *not* like Tony, who cheated on women, playing two at once.

At least she could be her own person with Max. She liked that. It was a positive step. She was never, never going to take the backward step of running home to her mother for help. For anything!

'Would you like me to drive you to another shopping mall?' Gerry asked as he saw her settled in the car.

She had forgotten the trolley containing the few pieces of fruit she had selected. They had walked out, leaving it standing in the aisle. 'Tomorrow afternoon,' she said, in too much emotional turmoil to think of food and knowing she could make do with what was available in the kitchenette. 'Let's go straight home, please, Gerry.'

He nodded and took the driver's seat without comment.

Home...tears pricked her eyes at that slip of the tongue. The children's house was not her home, yet it felt more like one than any of the places she'd lived in with her mother. Even the Randwick apartment that she and Tony had furnished had been more to his taste than hers—wanting to please him. He'd probably insist on keeping it as part of the divorce settlement. Chloe decided she didn't care. Sometime in the next two months she would find a place of her own and please herself with the furnishings.

It was difficult to keep blinking away the tears. Her chest was tight with them. Max had made it possible for her to put the past with her mother at a distance since Friday night, but meeting her face to face...she felt both physically and mentally drained by the effort of standing up to her, standing up for herself. She had run away from the confrontation in the end, with the help of the bodyguard Max had had the foresight to hire. Would she have managed otherwise?

She wasn't sure. The old sense of helplessness had welled up in her although she'd fought it as hard as she could. It wasn't easy to shed a lifetime of being dominated, being told what to do and torn up emotionally if she resisted, giving in because she couldn't bear the many manifestations of her mother's anger. She needed the refuge Max had given her, needed the time to build up her own strength of purpose. Yet was her mother right? Did Max have a personal as well as a professional motive for helping her? Was she hopelessly gullible? What was the truth?

The tears spilled over. She tried desperately to mop them up and regain some composure as they arrived at Max's mansion. Gerry opened the passenger door for her and she kept her head down while alighting from the car. 'Thank you,' she choked out, swallowing hard before adding, 'I'll see you in the morning, Gerry.'

'Have a good night, Miss Rollins,' he replied.

'You, too,' she mumbled and bolted for the children's house, wanting its cosy comfort to embrace her and close out all the horrid feelings aroused by the meeting with her mother.

Max felt his jaw tightening with anger as he listened to Gerry Anderson's report. Stephanie Rollins was obviously going to be relentless in her drive to get her cash-cow daughter back in her clutches. She was a shrewd operator, sowing doubts, fears and seeds of suspicion in Chloe's mind—everything possible to undermine trust in him. It was good that Chloe had defied her, but at what cost?

'The mother's a very nasty piece of work,' Gerry summed up. 'I'd say there's been physical as well as mental abuse in their relationship. I'm not into hitting women but I sure wanted to thump that one.'

'While I sympathise with the urge, be warned that she'd sue you for assault and manipulate the situation her way,' Max advised.

'Miss Rollins...' He shook his head. 'Something about her gets to me. You did good to rescue her from that woman.'

Doubts about his motives had been seeded in the bodyguard's mind, too. Max read them in the eyes scanning his, asking if he was going to be good for Chloe Rollins in the long run. Which was none of Gerry Anderson's business, and he knew it, so it wasn't put into words. But he cared—that *something* about Chloe would inspire it in most men—and the caring made him say, 'She was crying in the car. Don't know if there's anything you can do about it....'

'I can provide a distraction,' Max said with a reassuring smile. 'You may well be looking after a puppy at the studios tomorrow whenever Miss Rollins is required on set.'

The bodyguard's concern was swallowed up by a wide grin. 'No problem, Mr Hart. Got a dog of my own. Always liked them.'

The report over, they both stood and shook hands. The bodyguard made his exit from the library. Max sat back down on the chair behind his desk and thought about where he was going with Chloe Rollins. There was no question in his mind that he'd done her a good service by separating her from her mother. But would he be good for her in the long run?

He'd never asked that question of himself in his pursuit of other women. They'd always known the score with him and he hadn't ever felt responsible for the choice they made. But Chloe was different. She was very, very vulnerable. He had to take that into account or he might find it difficult to live with himself afterwards.

Chloe cringed at the knock on her door. She'd cleaned up her tear-blotched face, had a long, hot shower to ease the tension in her body, wrapped herself in the silk kimono she favoured for lounging around after working all day, and was curled up on the window seat in the living room, trying to empty her mind by watching the traffic on the harbour. She didn't want to see or talk to anyone, didn't want to think.

The knock was repeated.

Several times.

Becoming more insistent.

It forced her to realise that whoever it was probably knew she was home and would be concerned if she didn't appear. With a reluctant sigh, she uncurled herself, swung her feet onto the floor and headed for the door. Eric's weather-beaten face was almost pressed against one of the glass panes, relief replacing worry when he caught sight of her approach.

Chloe made a rueful grimace, indicating she wasn't dressed for receiving visitors, though she didn't mind speaking to the kindly old handyman who'd helped her move in here, opening and disposing of the boxes brought by the removalist. He was in his seventies, wiry in build and still surprisingly strong, his skin deeply tanned from working outdoors, though he always wore a cap to protect his bald head from getting sunburnt.

He smiled encouragingly at her, showing the yellowed teeth that had been discoloured from too many years of pipe-smoking. He was carrying a basket, loaded with bags—probably something he wanted to deliver to her. It wasn't until she was almost at the door that she saw he wasn't alone. A few paces behind him stood the unmistakable figure of Max Hart, his back turned to her, his head slightly bent as though he was studying the lawn.

Her heart instantly leapt into a faster beat, her hand lifting in agitation to the loose edges of the kimono gown near her breasts. *Her bare breasts.* She felt her nipples hardening as alarm jagged through her mind. If her mother was right about what Max wanted with her, she couldn't let him see her so readily naked in this gown. He might take it as an invitation. Besides, even though her body was covered, just his presence made her too acutely aware of it, too aware of his dynamic sexuality and how it affected her.

She gestured to Eric to wait and fled to her bedroom. Off with the robe, underclothes on, slacks, top, a quick brush through her hair and she was reasonably presentable. No make-up but that was good. It meant she wasn't trying to look attractive. She paused long enough to take several deep breaths, needing to calm herself, then went back to the front door, opening it without hesitation, speaking in an apologetic rush.

'Sorry to keep you waiting. I wasn't expecting anyone to call on me and...'

'Not to worry, Miss Chloe,' Eric assured her, grinning from ear to ear. 'We've brought you a little homecoming present.'

'A homecoming...?'

Eric stepped aside as Max turned to face her, and Chloe's bewilderment faded into a gasp of surprise at the sight of the tiny black-and-white puppy cradled in his arms.

'He's a miniature fox terrier,' Max said, smiling indulgently at the pup who was licking his hand. 'He looked at me through the pet shop window and his eyes said he needed someone to love him.' His gaze lifted from the pup, the dark brilliant eyes boring straight into Chloe's heart. 'I thought of you...saying yesterday you wanted something real in your life...'

'You bought him for me?' Delight was mixed with shame over letting her mother poison her thoughts about this man... her wonderful white knight providing her with everything she needed...never mind any dark side he might have.

'Do you want him?'

'Please…' She eagerly held out her arms and the adorable pup was quickly bundled into them. 'I wasn't ever allowed to have a pet. I'll love him to death, Max. Thank you so, so much!'

She hugged the squirming little body up against her shoulder and laughed as she felt her neck being licked.

'Got everything he needs here,' Eric said. 'Sleeping basket, food, bowls for water and food, collar and leash, dog shampoo…the whole works. Okay if I bring it in and show you everything?'

'Yes, please do.'

She stepped back inside to give him room to enter, expecting Max to follow. But he didn't. He stood in the doorway for a few moments, watching her petting the puppy, the sheer magnetism of the man making her pulse race and trapping her breath in her chest, and when he smiled directly at her, her mind felt positively giddy.

'Seeing your pleasure is my reward,' he said softly. 'I'll leave you to it, Chloe.'

He didn't wait for her to reply, striding away before she could find breath enough to speak. She told herself she had already thanked him anyway, but his departure and his wonderfully thoughtful gift left her feeling even more ashamed of letting her mother tarnish the image of him fighting her dragons.

She lifted the pup down from her shoulder to look into the eyes that had appealed to Max in the pet shop, asking to be loved. She saw the same expression in them and smiled. 'This is your home. With me,' she promised him.

And in that sweet moment of bonding with the beautiful little dog, she felt a huge welling of love for the man who had given her so much of what she'd needed, without demanding any more of her than fulfilling her contract with him as best she could.

CHAPTER SEVEN

THE rest of the working week passed without any upsetting incident. Chloe felt nervous about doing another shopping trip but she refused to be deterred from it, telling herself that would mean her mother was still dominating her life. She stocked up on her favourite foods and settled happily in the children's house each night, loving the company of her darling little dog. She saw nothing of Max, which made her even more comfortable with the situation, feeling it proved her mother was totally wrong about his motives for taking her under his protective wing.

Saturday was a glorious day, tempting her outside as soon as she'd done her washing and tidied the house. It was great fun taking her dog for a frolicking walk down to the lower terrace. He had to stop and sniff at everything, yapped wildly at finding a frog, and generally leapt around with the sheer joy of living. Chloe laughed at his antics, vastly amused when he'd tumble over, then quickly stand on stiff legs, looking around suspiciously as though to ask, 'What did that to me?' before bounding off again.

She ended up rolling on the grass with him, much to his

dancing excitement, and that was how Max came upon them on his way to the boatshed.

'Hi, there!' he called, startling Chloe into sitting bolt upright, which caused him to hastily add, 'Don't get up. It's good to see you looking so relaxed and I'm just passing by. It's such a perfect morning, I thought I'd take the catamaran out on the harbour.'

Like herself, he was wearing shorts and a T-shirt, and once again Chloe was struck by his awesome physique, her heart skittering, flutters in her stomach. He crouched down, his hands outstretched in open welcome as the puppy bounced across the grass to sniff him.

'Hi, little fella.' One hand was licked and Max used the other to scratch behind the dog's ear, smiling at Chloe as he did so. 'What did you call him?'

'Luther.'

'Luther,' he repeated in surprise, raising a quizzical eyebrow. 'That's a serious name for a playful pup.'

'It has dignity. He's only ever going to be little but he thinks he has dignity and I'm giving it to him.'

'Right!' Max grinned, highly amused by the idea. 'I can see that's important.'

'And he also reminded me of Martin Luther King.'

Both eyebrows shot up this time and Chloe grinned back at him as she explained, 'He's black and white and Martin Luther King fought for desegregation, wanting to bring blacks and whites together.'

'Ah! You've clearly given it a lot of thought.'

'A name deserves a lot of thought. You're loaded with it all your life.' She grimaced. 'I've always hated mine.'

He looked slightly bemused by this and asked, 'Why?'

She shook her head, not wanting to tell him it was how her

mother made such a harsh gutteral sound of it when she was angry. 'I just don't like it.'

'You could have it changed,' he advised her.

She shrugged. 'Too late for that. It's a career name now.'

'It's never too late to make changes,' he said seriously, straightening up and strolling towards her, Luther prancing around his feet. 'What name would you prefer for yourself?' he asked curiously.

'Maria.' It was soft and had a loving sound to it. 'Ever since I saw the musical *West Side Story*, I've wished it was mine, though I guess it wouldn't go so well with Rollins. Not as distinctive as Chloe.'

'Maria…' he repeated whimsically.

'And I ended up marrying a Tony,' she said with bitter irony. 'Just goes to show how dreams can lead you astray.'

'Well, you've woken up from that dream now, and Luther will give you more real devotion than your husband did.' He dropped down on his haunches to pet the pup again. 'Won't you, little fella?'

He was right about that. Nothing about Tony's devotion had been real. But that was behind her now, no point in dwelling on it. She had to look ahead. If she ever married again, she would make sure it was to a man of substance like…

Her gaze fastened on Max, who sprawled back on the grass, laughingly pretending that Luther had knocked him over. The pup leapt onto his chest and madly licked his chin. 'Save me! Call him off!' Max appealed to Chloe.

'Luther, come here!' she said firmly, and the little dog raced over to her, tail wagging like a windmill. She cuddled him on her lap, settling him down, eyeing Max with amusement as he rolled onto his side, propping himself up on his elbow. 'I don't think you needed to be rescued from a miniature fox terrier.'

His dark eyes twinkled teasingly. 'He was getting a taste for me. He might have gobbled me up.'

She laughed.

He smiled, and this close to her, his smile set off a fountain of buzzing female hormones inside Chloe. He was so attractive, for one wild moment, she fiercely envied Shannah Lian's intimate relationship with him, wishing she could experience him as a lover. Her mind instantly clamped down on the shockingly wayward thought and sought some normal distraction from it.

'Did you have a dog when you were a boy, Max?'

The smile turned into a sardonic grimace as he shook his head. 'The circumstances I lived in then…it wouldn't have been fair on a dog.'

Not fair on him, either, she thought. A drug-addicted mother would not have given him a stable life.

'I had a job on Sunday mornings for a while,' he said reminiscently. 'Pulling a barrow of newspapers around the neighbourhood, blowing a whistle for people to come out and buy. Their dogs always came out and I made friends with them. They'd follow me down the street until their owners called them back. I always enjoyed doing that paper run.'

'You've come a long way since then,' Chloe murmured.

'Yes. And still too much on the move to acquire a dog.'

Or a wife.

She wondered if those early years with his mother had taught him not to get attached to anyone or anything, to count only on himself. But this place had called to him.

'You have a home now,' she said.

'A home to come home to. I travel a lot, Chloe.'

'Do you ever get tired of it…the travelling?' she asked curiously.

'The flights can be tedious. Australia is a long way from anywhere else. But I like having the world as my playground. Not being limited.'

She sighed. 'You make me realise how limited my world has been. I haven't even been outside this country. My mother always had more work lined up for me, hardly ever a break.'

'You can change that, too.'

Yes, she could. Freedom was a powerful thing if she learnt to use it wisely.

'Have you ever been sailing, Chloe?'

'No.'

'Then come out on the catamaran with me,' he invited, his dark eyes challenging her to take on a new experience. 'We'll only be gone an hour or two and Eric will mind Luther. He's up on your terrace trimming the hedge.'

Max watched temptation war with caution. She wanted to accept, but undoubtedly her mother had fed her fears about being alone with the big, bad shark. The dog had made this little encounter safe, put her at ease, but without Luther…

She turned her gaze to the harbour. Her chin lifted slightly. Then with an air of self-determination, she looked back at him and said, 'You'll have to tell me what to do.'

'You don't have to do anything except sit or lie on the deck and enjoy skimming across the water,' he assured her, smiling as he pushed himself onto his feet. 'While you fix Luther up with Eric, I'll take the catamaran out to the wharf, ready for you to board.'

There was eager delight on her face as she scrambled up from the grass. 'I'll be as quick as I can.'

'No hurry. Get a hat, too, and put on some sun-block cream.'

'Okay.'

Max felt a zing of triumphant satisfaction as he headed down to the boatshed. Stephanie Rollins was fast losing her influence on Chloe. Which was all to the good. He wanted her to feel free, to make choices for herself, and she'd just chosen to be with him, despite the witch's warnings.

Once they were out in the harbour, Max realised winning had its downside. He had the exhilarating pleasure of watching Chloe's uninhibited joy in the speedy ride across the water, her laughter when waves splashed over the hull, leaving them both dripping wet. She didn't care about how she looked. She simply loved all the sensations of sailing. And it stoked Max's desire for her to the point of severe physical discomfort.

Several times he had to turn away from her, focus fiercely on manipulating the sail, changing the cat's direction, waiting until the tension in his groin eased. His baggy shorts gave him some cover but not enough after they'd got wet, and it certainly didn't help that Chloe's damp clothes clung to every luscious curve of her body.

He couldn't remember ever being on fire for a woman to this extent. He wanted to lick the salt water from her beautiful face, taste her laughter, peel off her clothes, bury his face in her breasts, suck the nipples that were poking out at him so teasingly, bury himself so deeply inside her nothing else would matter—all-consuming sex, devouring all the reasons why they shouldn't have it.

He knew she wasn't immune to his sexual attraction. The occasional sharp intake of breath, the quick look away, the self-conscious curling up of her long, bare legs—all revealing little actions. The big question was—would she fight what she wanted with him, or welcome it?

Risky business.

Rushing into it might break her trust in him.

But it was damned difficult to hold himself back.

At least another week, he told himself. Keep building the chemistry between them, breaking down the mental barriers, issuing tempting invitations, which would seem simply companionable, no reason to refuse—no reasonable reason.

'Had fun?' he asked as he brought the catamaran in beside the wharf, grabbing the ladder to hold the craft steady for Chloe to get off.

She glowed at him. 'It was brilliant, Max. Thank you so much.'

He grinned. 'Hungry work, sailing. Like to join me for lunch by the pool after you've cleaned up?'

Again the hesitation.

He pushed, teasingly adding, 'We can feed Luther tit-bits under the table.'

Including the dog sealed it.

She laughed. 'He loves chicken.'

'I'll ask Elaine to make us chicken caesar salads.'

'That would be great. You'll have two eager guests.'

'Glad to have the company.'

Chloe told herself it was stupid to deny herself the pleasure of *his* company. He was a brilliant, fascinating man. The powerful tug of his strong masculinity would affect any woman. It wasn't special to her. She just had to learn to deflect it, concentrate on their conversation. This was a chance to learn more about him and his life and she wanted to know how he'd managed the journey he'd taken to here, what it took to become the man he was.

It was the right decision to go. The lunch was delicious. Max was totally relaxed, enjoying Luther's appetite for chicken as well as his own. Chloe had tied a sarong over her swimming costume, and relieved of being over-conscious of her body in his presence, she relaxed, too. Max had already been in the pool for a swim when she'd arrived and had a towel tucked around his waist—a decent enough covering to allay the unsettling awareness of *his* body.

Luther curled up on one of the lounges and went to sleep while they lingered at the table, finishing off the bottle of wine Edgar had brought with their lunch. Chloe screwed up her courage to do some probing into Max's background, telling herself it was okay if he rebuffed her. He had a right to his privacy. She could apologise and backtrack into neutral subjects.

'Max, I know your mother died of a drug overdose when you were sixteen. You must have been through worse things than me in your growing up years,' she started off, her eyes earnestly appealing for his forbearance when she saw the shutting down of all expression on his face. 'I just want to know how you moved past it.'

He turned his gaze away from her, eyelids lowered to half-mast. For several tense moments, Chloe sensed him brooding over whether to answer her or not, his mind travelling back to the past, sifting through it, weighing up whether he was prepared to reveal anything. When he finally spoke, it was in a very dry, dismissive tone.

'When you have nothing, you have nothing to lose. You move on because there's no alternative.' He looked back at her, his eyes very dark and intense. 'You have the harder road to travel, Chloe. You know there's someone you can retreat to if you find it too difficult. That may weaken your resolve to move on.'

'I'll never go back to my mother,' she said vehemently, knowing she had been weak not to make the break before this. The feeling of being hopelessly trapped in a relentless cycle of demands was gone now, thanks to Max.

He smiled. 'I hope not. Today I've seen a vitality in you that was missing when you were yourself, not playing a role for the camera.'

He made her feel more alive than she'd ever been. This wasn't make-believe, escaping from reality. It was how she actually felt here and now. 'Did you daydream as a kid, Max?'—escaping his realities?

'No. I watched television. I absorbed television. I didn't have a normal bed-time and it blocked out my mother's crazy stuff. I'd sit there working out why one show had more popular appeal than another. Was it the storyline? Was it the actors? Was it the camera work? What would I do to make it better?' His eyes twinkled in mocking amusement at having turned a bad time into something good. 'Probably the best preparation for what I do now—judging what viewers will like and what they won't, getting the right cast and the right crew to give a show optimum appeal.'

'But you didn't start off in television,' Chloe remarked, puzzled that he hadn't headed straight for it, given his intense interest.

He shook his head. 'I didn't want to be an odd-job boy at a television studio, which was all I could have been in that industry at sixteen.'

'You might have been cast in a show if you'd tried out for

one.' He certainly had the male x-factor that was very marketable in television.

'I didn't want to be an actor. I wanted to run the show, Chloe, be in control.'

Master of his own fate, she thought. Had the drive for control been born in him or was it a reaction to the out-of-control life his mother had led? Her own life had been so overwhelmingly controlled, any overt rebellion crushed by abusive tirades, she'd lost the spirit to even try for any control. Until Max had stepped in. She fiercely resolved to be mistress of her own fate after she left here.

'Getting a job at a publishing house was a stepping stone to the big picture,' he went on. 'It was the same field—selling stories, appealing to what people wanted whether it was fiction or non-fiction. I made it to marketing manager by the time I was eighteen. Which opened doors for me to get where I wanted to be.'

Chloe didn't know his exact age—somewhere in his late thirties. It was an amazing accomplishment to have risen from nothing to a billionaire television baron. 'It must give you a tremendous sense of satisfaction, having achieved the wealth and power to choose what shows you want to produce,' she remarked admiringly.

'Mmm...' Ruthless purpose flashed into his eyes. '*My* way.'

'Like getting me for the lead role in this show,' she murmured, remembering what he'd told her. 'You didn't care how much my mother haggled over the contract.'

His mouth quirked and the expression in his eyes simmered into something else—something that made her heart skip and sent tingles along every nerve. 'I wanted you,' he said.

On the surface it was a professional comment but it didn't

feel like one. She quickly lowered her gaze and covered her inner confusion by picking up her almost empty glass of wine and slowly finishing it off. Was she hearing what she wanted to hear, seeing what she wanted to see? Max was in a relationship with another woman—a stunningly beautiful woman who was probably as self-assured as he was. Why would a man like him find a lame duck like herself desirable?

Apart from which, she shouldn't be excited by the idea that the attraction she felt with him was returned. It made her situation here perilously close to her mother's nasty reading of it. Although Max had made no move on her. Not even the suggestion of a move. They were just talking. Which was what she should be doing instead of thinking.

'What was your favourite show when you were a boy, Max?' she asked, forcing herself to look at him with curious interest.

'*M*A*S*H*,' he answered without hesitation. 'The script was brilliant, the cast of characters was brilliantly balanced, the acting was superb, and it could make you laugh and cry and tug at every emotion in between. I loved that show.'

Love…she could hear it in his voice and wondered if he'd ever loved a woman with the same fervour, loving everything about her.

'Did it get to you, too?' he asked.

Chloe had to drag her mind back to the conversation. She shook her head. 'I've never seen it. My mother dictated what I watched.'

He grimaced, then looked consideringly at her. 'Would you like to see some of it? I have the whole collection of *M*A*S*H* in my library. I could give you the first season's episodes to watch and if you enjoy them…'

'Yes, please.' Chloe jumped up eagerly, seizing the opportunity to end the foolish meandering in her mind. 'Could we go and get the discs now, Max? The activity this morning and the wine over lunch… I'm feeling drowsy so I want to head off for an afternoon nap. But I'd love to see what you saw in *M*A*S*H* when I wake up.'

He nodded agreeably, rising from his chair, and she quickly collected Luther, who was still asleep. The excursion to Max's library only took ten minutes. It was an amazing library, the shelves more stocked with CD discs of movies and television shows than books, although there were stacks of them, as well. Max moved straight to the *M*A*S*H* collection, handed her a set of discs and invited her to exchange them for others anytime she liked. Chloe thanked him and quickly took her leave.

She *was* tired and she did go to sleep, driving off the madly mixed-up thoughts of Max by reading a book until her eyelids drooped. Luther's yapping woke her, the insistent noise bringing her slowly out of deep slumber. She rolled over on the bed, intending to scoop the dog up to cuddle him back into silence, then realised the yapping was coming from the living room.

Frowning over what might have disturbed the little dog, she pushed herself off the bed, automatically re-covering herself with the silk kimono she'd donned for her afternoon siesta and tying the belt securely as she walked out of the bedroom.

And stopped dead.

A face was peering through the glass panes of the front door, a face she never wanted to see again—the face of Tony Lipton!

CHAPTER EIGHT

As Chloe stared at him in stunned disbelief, Tony caught sight of her and with an air of triumphant satisfaction, stepped back, his hand reaching for the door-knob, which turned because she hadn't switched on the locking mechanism. It had completely slipped her mind—being with Max, thinking of Max. Apart from which, she was supposed to be safe on Max's property.

The door opened and Tony was in before Chloe could do or say anything to stop him. 'I wasn't sure I had the right place with that damned dog here,' he said, casting a malevolent look at Luther, who was still yapping and jumping at his legs as though to drive him out again.

Good dog, Chloe thought, wishing she had the physical strength to evict her highly unwelcome husband. 'You have no right to be in this house, Tony,' she threw at him in bitter resentment.

He glowered at her. 'You're still my wife, and Maxa-million-bucks Hart has no right to come between us.'

'You didn't mind Laura Farrell coming between us.'

He waved a sharply dismissive hand. 'That was nothing.'

'I don't call a baby nothing.'

He rearranged his expression to apologetic appeal. 'If you'll just hear me out, Chloe…'

'I don't want to listen to another pack of lies from you. Which is why I took up Max's offer of this house. What I would like to know is how you got past his security.'

He smirked. 'I came by boat, snuck under his wharf to avoid triggering any alarm, climbed up the rock breakwater and beat his bloody security.'

'Then I'd advise you to leave the same way or I'll call the main house and you'll get charged with trespassing.'

'You won't call anyone, Chloe.' He moved quickly to stand between her and the telephone, which he must have spotted on the kitchen bench. He held up both hands in a non-threatening gesture. 'I just want to talk with you. Given the years we've had together, I think I deserve the chance to…'

'No!' she cut in decisively, determined not to be moved by any persuasion he tried. 'Our marriage is over, Tony. I won't change my mind about that no matter what you say.'

The hands turned palm out in appeal. 'I know you're upset and you have good reason to be, but…' He huffed and frowned down at Luther, who'd ceased yapping to sink his teeth into one of Tony's trouser legs and was trying to tug him towards the door. 'Will you call this son of a bitch off? He's ruining my trousers.'

'I do not appreciate your calling my dog nasty names. He's simply doing his best to protect me from an intruder and I don't give a damn about your trousers,' she said, folding her arms belligerently. 'It's you who should call this off and go, Tony.'

'*Your* dog?' He looked sharply at her. 'Since when did you acquire a dog?'

'Since I walked away from the people who didn't want me to have a pet. Namely you and my mother.'

'It's not practical for you to have a pet,' he argued.

'Not practical for me to have a baby, either.'

Recognising that appeasement was his only favourable course in the face of proven infidelity, he backed down, hands lifted in surrender this time. 'Okay...okay...' He tried one of his winning smiles. 'It's fine by me if you want to keep the dog. Look...I'll make friends with him. What's his name?'

Chloe did not back down. Nothing on earth would make her back down. 'You don't need to know his name. You're not going to be part of his life.'

Tony ignored this assertion and crouched down, arranging his face in an indulgent expression as he reached out to pat Luther. 'Hello, little guard-dog,' he crooned. 'You're doing a good job but you've got the wrong guy. I'm a friend.'

Luther had great instincts. He didn't believe Tony for a second. He growled at being touched by the enemy, released the trouser leg, snapped his head around and sunk his teeth into Tony's wrist.

'Bloody hell! He bit me!' It was a cry of angry outrage.

Serve him right, Chloe thought with vicious satisfaction, trying to fool a dog like he'd thought he'd fooled her throughout their marriage. The blinkers had fallen off her eyes long ago on that score. No way could Tony charm her into believing anything or *doing* anything for him anymore.

But it was she who cried out as he shook Luther off, grabbed the dog's wildly squirming body, strode to the door, yanked it open, hurled the little terrier outside and closed the door on him. She flew at Tony, fists beating at his chest as he stood in front of the door, preventing her from reversing his action.

'How dare you treat Luther like that, you rotten bully!' she yelled at him. 'Get out of my way! Get out of my life!'

'You've completely lost the plot, Chloe!' he fiercely retorted, grabbing her wrists to stop the pummelling. 'Calm down! All I want is a civilised conversation without a rabid dog distracting us and that's what we're going to have.'

'Let me go!' she screamed, struggling to pull out of his hold.

He forcibly hauled her over to the sofa and flung her onto it. 'Sit there and shut up!' he commanded, all primed to prevent her from moving, glaring down at her with meanly narrowed eyes.

Chloe obeyed, frightened he might do her worse violence if she tried to escape him. She sat still and retreated into grim silence, staring stonily at him as he pulled one of the rockers around so he could sit in face-to-face confrontation with her. Fear was pounding through her heart but she refused to show it. Tony's behaviour was utterly contemptible. Yet the sense of being trapped again was eating at her mind, and all she could think of was how much she needed to be rescued.

Luther was madly yapping outside.

Was Eric still working somewhere in the grounds?

Would he hear the little dog's distress and wonder?

But it wasn't Eric her mind fixed on. She wanted Max to come—Max, her white knight, who'd been standing between her and her dragons, keeping them away.

Max decided the only way to get rid of this continually niggling frustration over Chloe was with a burst of intense physical activity—swim twenty lengths of the pool without a pause. It might also cool down the long-simmering desire she hadn't wanted to know about. He kept remembering her reaction when he'd let her see it, the swift lowering of her eyes, the agitated reach for her glass of wine, then seizing the first reasonable opportunity to part from his company.

She wasn't ready for him and Max wasn't used to waiting. In the ordinary course of events, the women he connected with were only too eager to get into bed with him. No reservations at all. The problem was this situation was not ordinary. The connection *was* there with Chloe. He didn't doubt that for a second. But she clearly had emotional issues, which were making her shy away from acknowledging the sexual buzz between them, let alone showing pleasure in it.

Did it frighten her?

Did she think it was too soon after her husband's defection to be feeling anything towards another man?

Max didn't give a hoot how scandalous an affair between them might be, but it could be worrying Chloe. Though surely she realised he would look after her, and on a purely practical level, there were many advantages in being attached to him. It certainly wouldn't do her career any harm. He could find the best roles for her to play, take her places she'd never been, show her the world and show *her* to the world.

Unfortunately he suspected she didn't have a worldly streak in her, and she was certainly not driven by ambition, which made her very different to most of the women he met. He'd recognised that from the start and found it very appealing. She'd been *used*, and suffered so much from it she'd never use anyone else to push her own barrow. He couldn't change her feelings in that regard and didn't want to. He just wanted...*her*.

Too much.

Too soon.

He headed out to the pool. The heat of the day was lingering on. Maybe Chloe would feel hot after her nap and come up for a swim. He wanted her so badly even a *limited* encounter with her was better than nothing. He'd no sooner stepped out on the pool patio than he heard Luther yapping in frantic ferocity for a little dog.

Something was wrong. Max instantly broke into a fast stride under the columned pergola that led to the steps down to the next terrace. It had been a bad summer for snakes. Eric had spotted a few on the property—harmless green tree snakes—but it didn't mean there weren't any red-bellied black ones around. Or a deadly brown one. Terriers were renowned for going after snakes. If Luther got bitten…

But why wasn't Chloe calling him off? Surely she hadn't let the dog out alone. He was only a pup—eight weeks old. Yet there was no sound from her. This felt like a bad scene. Adrenaline was pumping through him as the guest house came into view. Luther was clawing at the front door in a desperate frenzy. No Chloe in sight.

Max bounded down the steps. Luther didn't even register his approach. The little dog's attention was totally fixed on whatever was going on inside the house. Had Chloe fainted, collapsed, knocked herself out somehow?

A sense of urgency drove him into running to the front door, hand reaching instantly for the knob, testing if it was locked. It wasn't. It turned. Both he and Luther burst into the living room, the dog belting straight for the man leaping up from one of the rocking chairs. Chloe was huddled on the far corner of the sofa, her face lighting with huge relief at seeing him.

The man turned, scowling at Luther, his expression sliding to angry defiance as he saw Max.

Tony Lipton!

With her husband distracted from her, Chloe pushed up from the sofa, ran around the chair he had occupied and threw herself at Max, who was only too happy to curl a protective arm around her and hold her close, so close he could feel the agitated rise and fall of her lovely soft breasts and the rapid thumping of her heart. He rubbed his cheek against her silky hair—too tempting not to—and glared at Tony Lipton over her head, hating him for having had an intimate relationship with Chloe and not even valuing it enough to care about her.

'How did you get here?' he demanded.

Chloe answered in a wild rush. 'He came by boat, Max, and he threw Luther out and forced me to sit down and listen to him. I tried to make him go, but…'

'*Forced?*' Anger surged, the urge to punch out Tony Lipton rising to flash-point.

Fear flickered in the other man's eyes. 'Oh, for God's sake! She's making a drama out of nothing. I just wanted to talk to her,' he jeered dismissively. 'I have a right to, as her husband.'

'No-one has the right to abuse someone else's rights,' Max shot back at him contemptuously, reining in the wildly violent streak this situation had tapped. Control had been the key to the life he had achieved for himself, gaining it, holding it, never letting it slip. That *something about Chloe* was affecting his judgement, stirring feelings that made him a stranger to himself—jealousy, hatred, savagery. He sternly checked himself and spoke with icy control. 'This is my property. Chloe is my guest. She wants you to leave and I will not have that wish disregarded.'

'A lot more than a guest by the look of it,' came the rash retort, his eyes raking over Max's almost naked body, belligerently ignoring the aggression he was inciting.

It was suddenly clear to Max that Tony wanted to goad him into a physical fight regardless of any injury to himself, wanted to make an accusation of assault, milk another sensational story out of the situation. No way was Max about to oblige him. He wouldn't lower himself to gutter behaviour no matter what the provocation.

'Get out, Tony. Get out while the going is still good. You can't stop me from calling the police and having you charged for trespass, and if you continue to stalk Chloe, I'll have a court order issued to legally prevent you from coming anywhere near her. It won't be her name or mine dragged through mud. It will be yours.'

Tony's hands clenched into fists. He glowered at Max, hating his power, wanting to somehow bring him down. 'Chloe is my wife,' he said as though that exonerated his behaviour.

Chloe twisted around to hurl her own response at him. 'I told you our marriage is over. I'm never coming back to you. Never!'

'Because *he's* filled your head with other options,' he yelled back at her, shaking an accusing finger at Max. 'You're a fool to trust him, Chloe. Once he's had what he wants from you, he'll dump you like he dumps all his women.'

'I don't care!' she snapped. 'He gives me what I need, and even if it is only a short-term thing, I'd rather be with him than you.'

Elation spilled through Max's mind. She had just made an active choice. He'd won. All he had to do now was get rid of the hanging-on husband.

'Give it up, Tony,' he tersely advised. 'You're in a no-win situation. Leave now or I'll call the police.'

Luther, who'd lined himself up with Max and Chloe, growled his own warning.

Tony turned his vitriol onto him. 'Bloody dog!'

Luther charged, teeth bared to take a chunk of the enemy. Tony kicked him viciously right across the room. Chloe screamed and ran to check the little dog for injury.

Max's control snapped. With Chloe's scream reverberating through his head and outrage at the callous cruelty to a little pup pumping through his heart, he took one step forward and king-hit Tony Lipton on the jaw. The sight of him, sprawled on the floor near the door, still despoiling the children's house that should have been a safe refuge, could not be borne. Max grabbed the back of his shirt collar and dragged him outside, dropping him on the lawn before quickly returning to the living room to see how Luther was.

'Do we need to call a vet?' he asked Chloe, who was cradling the little dog on her lap.

'I don't think anything's broken,' she answered anxiously. 'I think he just tumbled, Max.'

'I'll look him over as soon as I get back from dumping Tony in his boat.'

'You needn't dump him gently,' she said with vehement feeling.

A fierce exhilaration zinged through Max as he headed back to her decisively *ex*-husband, who had managed to draw himself up on his hands and knees, shaking his head dazedly. It might not have been a wise move, punching out Tony Lipton, but he couldn't bring himself to regret it. Justice had been served, albeit in a primitive fashion, and he'd certainly not damaged himself in Chloe's eyes.

He grabbed Tony's collar again and the waistband of his trousers, lifted him onto his feet, and began frog-marching him across the lawn to the steps leading to the bottom terrace.

'Let me go! Let me go!' he gurgled, arms flailing as he tried to balance himself.

'You used force on Chloe and force on her dog. Have a taste of it yourself,' Max said, using unrelenting strength to push him along.

'I'll get you for this! You've broken my jaw.'

'No witnesses,' Max mocked.

'Chloe…'

'Will not testify on your behalf. You kicked her dog.'

They reached the steps and Tony struggled against Max's grip. 'All right! All right! I'm going! Just get your hands off me.'

'Okay. But try anything stupid and I'll throw you down the entire flight.'

Max let him stumble down the steps by himself, following to ensure Tony did, in fact, leave the property. He'd tied his boat to a pole at the base of the wharf—a small hired outboard motorboat—hidden by the rock breakwater. Max watched him clamber into it, untie the rope, start the motor and head out into the harbour. Neither man said goodbye.

Max waited until the boat was completely out of sight. He didn't think Tony Lipton would be returning in a hurry. Nevertheless, he made a mental note to have the security system tightened up on his harbour frontage. There should not have been a loophole for an intruder to scramble through. He'd failed Chloe on that count. If she now felt unsafe in the guest house, would she be willing to move into the mansion with him?

One step at a time, Max told himself. He had to get back to her now, seize whatever advantage he could from the positive flow of emotion towards him—ride the wave of opportunity.

He'd taken quite a few steps before it struck him he'd be breaking his own rules if he invited Chloe to share his own living quarters. In all his relationships with women, he'd never co-habited with any one of them, consciously avoiding any claim of a de facto wife partnership that could demand a financial settlement at the end of the affair. He hadn't wanted a wife, hadn't wanted a woman to fill that role in his life and he'd always made that quite clear.

That special something about Chloe was blurring all the rules that made his life what it had become. He'd just acted completely out of character. He should be appalled at his loss of control, not savouring the satisfaction it had given him. Life with his mother had been chaos and he'd hated it. Order, logic, a sane approach to everything…that was *his* safety net. He had to move with care where Chloe was concerned. Satisfying his desire for her was one thing, leading into an area of heavy commitment quite another.

But the only future he had to think of right now was this time with her and he was going to make the most of it.

CHAPTER NINE

LUTHER curled up on her lap and went to sleep, probably a normal reaction to frantic activity and shock. Chloe hoped so. He was only a baby and slept a lot in the normal course of events. She kept stroking him lightly, wanting to soothe away any lingering trauma. Such a brave little dog, and his wild yapping had brought Max to her when she'd desperately needed some strong intervention.

Max, in his brief black swimming costume, looking like a Greek god with all his physical power on display—her saviour once again. She hadn't cared that he was almost naked. It hadn't worried her one bit having her body hugged against his. If she was honest with herself, she'd revelled in his muscular support and was savagely glad he'd hit Tony and hauled him away. If they were living in some primitive society, she would certainly want Max as her mate. In fact, she would be happy to share a cave with him in every sense.

But their lives weren't so simple. Hers, particularly, was complicated with a whole lot of issues, and she shouldn't keep leaning on Max to fix everything for her. Apart from which, he was currently attached to another woman, and she shouldn't be forgetting that relationship, either. Although she was feeling more and more connected to him on many levels, and the plain truth was she wanted him to want her, regardless of every other issue.

Was that weak and stupid?

She didn't know, didn't have time to sort it out. Max strode back into the children's house, filling it with his powerful presence, and her mind went to mush. He was a marvellous man—a dangerous, ruthless, infinitely desirable man—and she wanted to fling herself at him again, feel his arms around her, crushing her body against his, feel everything he could make her feel.

Did he see that wild, wanton desire in her eyes? For one heart-stopping moment, he paused, his dark riveting gaze holding hers, questioning, probing with an intensity that trapped the breath in her throat. Then he looked down at the little dog in her lap and moved forward, crouching down beside her.

'He seems to be breathing normally.'

Which was more than she could say for herself. Her lungs relaxed back into action and she managed to speak normally. 'He whimpered for a while, but I couldn't feel anything broken.'

'I think Tony's foot went more under Luther's belly than connecting with his ribs, but if you'd like me to call a vet…'

She shook her head. 'I'll wait until he wakes up, see how he is then.'

'Where's his sleeping basket?'

'In the corner next to the doll house. He likes it there.'

'Don't get up. I'll fetch it and you can gently transfer him.'

Luther barely stirred as she lifted him into the basket, only opening his eyes to check all was as it should be then closing them again. Max carried the basket back to the corner as

Chloe pushed up from the floor. Acutely conscious of her own nakedness underneath the silk kimono, she re-adjusted it to maximum modesty as Max moved the rocker Tony had occupied back to its correct position and closed the front door, scanning the room to see if anything else had been changed.

'Are you going to feel nervous staying here now, Chloe?' he asked with a look of sharp concern.

'No. I'm sure Tony won't come back.' She grimaced. 'It was my fault he got in. I forgot to lock the door before lying down for a nap.'

'It was not your fault,' he retorted vehemently. 'Tony had no right to do what he did.'

'I know. I know. I just meant…' She gestured apologetically. 'I was careless, Max. I'm sorry you had to come and rescue me again.'

'The fault is not yours,' he repeated, shaking his head as he walked over to her. 'You've been a victim for a long time, Chloe. You have to stop that kind of thinking and take a clear look at where you are and why.'

His hands curled around her shoulders, fingers gently kneading her tense muscles. His eyes blazed with a dark fire that seemed to sear her soul. 'You said you wanted to be with me,' he reminded her. 'Was that because I saved you or…?'

She didn't consciously lift her hands to his bare chest. They seemed to have been drawn there and she didn't want to pull them away from the warmth and strength of his intense masculinity. She wanted to go on touching him, feeling him, although she was quivering inside at her own boldness in making this physical contact with him. The look in his eyes was tugging at her, too, demanding a response with almost mesmerising power. Some part of her mind knew he wouldn't take unless she was willing to give, yet another part wanted him to take, removing all responsibility from her.

The weak part.

The victim part.

And with that awful recognition came a sudden surge of rebellious determination to be more assertive where her own wishes were concerned. 'It's not just gratitude I feel for you,' she said. 'And I don't want it to be just a protective thing you feel for me,' she added recklessly. 'I want…'

She couldn't bring herself to voice it out loud—all the wildly tumbling desires creating havoc inside her.

'This, Chloe?' he murmured, his eyes glittering knowingly as he slid one hand up her throat, his thumb tilting her chin up, his fingers stroking her cheek.

Her lips parted but not to speak, to draw in breath because she desperately needed it.

'This?' he repeated, his head bending towards hers.

Yes, yes, careened around her mind.

His lips brushed hers, raising a host of electric tingles, which were quickly soothed into softer, more seductive sensations as he moved into tasting them, tugging lightly on the sensitive inner tissues, sliding his tongue over them—a gentle, mesmerising kissing that held Chloe totally captivated, craving more.

Her hands slid up over his shoulders, around his neck, fingers eagerly thrusting into his hair, clasping his head to keep it lowered to hers, blindly encouraging a deeper intimacy to feed the hungry desire racing through her veins, arousing needs that had never really been answered.

Almost instantly a strong arm encircled her waist, scooping her into full body contact with him, her breasts exulting in the hot pressure of his wonderfully masculine chest, her thighs revelling in the rocklike support of his, her stomach contracting excitedly at being furrowed by his sexual arousal, her mind lost in a tumultuous sea of elation at knowing that her own wanting was returned in full measure.

And his kiss was much deeper now, a marauding exploration of her mouth that incited her into invading his, their tongues tangling with a passionate intensity that shot wild excitement through her entire body. She couldn't get enough of him. A moan of gut-wrenching need dragged from her throat when his mouth broke from hers to draw in breath.

'Chloe…' It was a gasp, a groan, a sound he blew into her ear, making it tingle with an explosion of sensation.

She buried her face into the curve of his shoulder and neck, her lips grazing over his skin, tasting him, finding the pulse at the base of his throat, instinctively sucking on it, wanting his heart beating for her. His head jerked back. His hands clutched her bottom, squeezing her flesh closer to his, and just as she wished there was nothing preventing skin-to-skin contact, he growled and jackknifed forward, scooping her off her feet, whirling her up and into the bedroom, his chest heaving, his breathing harsh.

He stood her beside the bed, tugged the tie-belt of her kimono apart and slid the silk gown off her shoulders, following the glide of the fabric with his mouth, kissing the bared skin, making her shiver with delicious anticipation for what he might do to her when she was fully naked. As his hands drew the sleeves down her arms, his lips trailed a hot steamy path to her breasts, his tongue swirling around each stiffened peak, making them bullet-hard, shooting an arc of sweetly aching sensation to below her stomach.

She was barely conscious of the robe dropping to the floor, pooling around her feet. Her entire body was focused on what he was making her feel. Then his arms were around her, crushing her wet breasts to his chest, and one of his hands was thrusting up the curve of her spine to the nape of her neck, fingers threading through her hair. She lifted her face to his and his mouth crashed onto hers with swift devouring force, instantly inciting a passionate response.

Her arms wrapped themselves around his waist, hugging him tightly. The frenzied kissing stirred an intense frustration that he was not as naked as she was. Her hands dived down to hook her thumbs under the hip band of his swimming costume and drag them over the taut cheeks of his buttocks. She had to wrench her mouth from his to finish the task of peeling off this last barrier between them. Dropping into a crouch to pull the costume down his muscular thighs, she goggled at the size of his erection, fascinated by how much bigger it was than Tony's. *Everything* about Max was so different, so powerful, so incredibly exciting.

He lifted his feet for her to whip this last piece of clothing away. His hands were tangled in her hair, wanting to tug her upright again, but Chloe paused, drawn to do what Tony had always expected of her although with Max she really wanted to, swirling her tongue around the swollen head of his penis, encircling it with her lips, drawing it slowly into her mouth, savouring the tight, velvety skin.

'No, don't!' Max cried out, bending to grab her arms and haul her up to face him, his eyes glittering with agonised need.

Confused by his rejection of the intimacy, Chloe gabbled out, 'I'm sorry. I thought you'd like it. Tony…'

'I'm not Tony!' he said savagely. 'I don't want to be serviced by you, Chloe. I want *you*. And I'm so on fire for you, if I let you keep doing that…yes, I like it but not now. Not when I want all of you first.'

Again he crushed her to him, moving to the bed, kneeling over her as he lowered her onto it, passionate purpose blazing from his eyes. 'I want to feel all of you, taste all of you, know all of you, watch your face as we come together.'

Her mind reeled at the intensity of his desire for her. She felt it resonating through her in the ravaging depth of his kiss, in the way he set her on fire when he sucked on her breasts, her back arching to the intoxicating heat of his mouth, her flesh burning under his mouth as he moved it slowly, erotically, down her body, her stomach tightening with almost painful tension when he reached the apex of her thighs, parting her legs, stroking the soft hidden folds of her sex, kissing her *there*, licking her most sensitive place with delicate flicks of his tongue, an exquisite torture that she could hardly bear but didn't want stopped.

She lay with her hands clenched at her sides, trying to hold on, feeling her insides quivering towards some cataclysmic meltdown. Her eyes were closed, every ounce of concentration focused on what was happening to her. She forgot to breathe until her chest grew so tight it threatened to burst and she sucked in quick little gusts of air. It had never been like this for her, never, never, never…so incredible, so agonisingly blissful.

She felt the last threads of her control starting to snap, tension breaking up, trembling on the edge of chaos, and her hands uncurled and flew into his hair, fingers scrabbling, pulling, wildly insistent words pouring from her mouth. 'Stop… please…you must… I need you to come into me now…now…'

His strength filling her before she fell apart…his power making everything right…

He surged up, plucking her hands from his hair, slamming them into the pillow on either side of her head. 'Look at me, Chloe!' he commanded.

Her body was frantically poised for more direct action, her head threshing around in mindless need, but her eyes did snap open and she tried to focus on the face looming over hers— a harshly strained face, a darkly handsome face, with brilliant black eyes blazing down at her, demanding something from her, she didn't know what, couldn't think, but his name spilled from her lips in a husky cry of need.

'Max…'

'Yes…' It sounded like a rasp of satisfaction, then another command. 'Wrap your legs around me, Chloe. Take me as I take you.'

Her legs felt weak and shaky. Max released her hands and helped her, lifting her knees, and then it was easy, her ankles hooking together.

Holding him, having him encircled by her legs, actively offering the other more intimate encirclement…it felt wickedly wonderful, and she was dying to take him, all of him.

'Keep your eyes open,' he insisted.

She stared up at him, willing him to go on, desperate for him to give himself to her. A gasp fell from her lips as she felt his hard flesh push slowly into her slippery softness. Her inner muscles started convulsing, urgently wanting him deeper. Her heart was going crazy, heat racing through her veins, her face aglow with it, her whole body simmering, seething towards some unimaginable flash-point.

He went deeper. Her chest tightened up. She panted for

breath. Her head felt as though it was splitting apart. Her eyes glazed over, losing their focus. And still he moved further inside her, deeper than she'd ever experienced, and it was so achingly sweet to be filled with him, so… Her head arched back and a cry tore from her throat as everything inside her seemed to erupt in an ecstatic fountain of exquisite pleasure. Her head swam into a blissfully dreamy state and she looked at Max, who had done this amazing thing, her eyes filled with awed wonder.

He smiled a slow benevolent smile, his dark brilliant eyes tenderly caressing her as he leaned down and filled her mouth with his in a long, delicious kiss that heightened the lovely sensations floating through her.

'Thank you,' she whispered as he drew back.

He shook his head, his eyes still smiling. 'It's not over.'

He started rocking back and forth inside her with a gentle rhythm, watching her face, and to Chloe's astonishment the floating sea of pleasure he had taken her to gathered waves that rolled through her, building up to one ecstatic peak after another, not as explosive as the first, but just as glorious in the intensity of feeling. And her heart swelled with love for him and what he was doing to her.

She watched his face as the surges inside her became more powerful, the rhythm faster, the smile swallowed up by tension, the need for release turning his eyes an opaque black. He threw his head back, too, and cried out as the shuddering spasms of climax sent their flood of pleasure through him.

His chest was heaving for breath as he collapsed forward, arms burrowing under her, rolling onto his back and carrying her with him, holding her in a fiercely possessive embrace. She lay with her head tucked under his chin, her hand spread over his thundering heart, her legs limply sprawled over his, and felt a strange wave of tenderness, wanting to soothe him into the same lovely sense of contentment he'd given her. Was it over now, she wondered, or was this the beginning of an intimacy that would move her life to a place she had never imagined?

Her mind drifted to the image she had once had of him—Maximilian Hart, the powerful, ruthless, intimidating mover and shaker who always got what he wanted. The master player. He'd moved her, shaken the whole foundations of her world, but what, in the end, did he want with her?

Right now, Chloe couldn't bring herself to care.

She loved being with him like this.

And she was going to revel in it as long as it lasted.

CHAPTER TEN

MAX let himself bask in her soft ministrations, his mind still revelling in how she had responded to him—the excitement rippling through her body, the look of incredulous wonder on her face, the unequivocal seizures of intense pleasure. He had no doubt she'd never felt anything quite so climactic before, which gave him an enormous sense of satisfaction. Her rotten husband had obviously been a selfish lover—selfish in everything. It elated him that this sexual experience had been a revelation to her, that *he* had given her what she should have been given.

He wove his fingers through the silky tresses of her hair, loving the feel of it—soft like a baby's. Which reminded him. It had been totally reckless to go ahead without using a condom. The dog had brought him here. He hadn't come prepared for sex. But when he'd seen desire shining in Chloe's incredibly eloquent eyes, he hadn't cared about anything else, not even when it had flitted through his mind that she could fall pregnant. That cautionary bit of sanity had been crowded out by wild thoughts of taking care of her and the child, marrying her if need be—anything but putting her off having what he wanted, too.

He should check if there was any danger of pregnancy. He didn't really want that complication. It forced issues that shouldn't be forced. He didn't know how far he wanted to go with Chloe, but he knew the journey was better travelled free and clear of having to consider the life of an innocent child.

'Chloe…' His voice came out in a gravelly tone. He swallowed to clear his throat.

'Mmmh?' It was a contented hum, nothing fretting at her mind.

Which was good, Max told himself. 'I didn't plan this and I had no protection with me,' he said, unable to wipe all concern from his mind.

'S'okay,' she assured him dreamily.

'It's safe?' he persisted, needing that fact nailed down.

'Mmmh.' She sucked in a deep breath and explained, 'I'm in the middle of a month of contraceptive pills. Didn't think I should go off them until the end of the prescription. Just as well,' she added on a carefree sigh.

'Yes. Just as well,' he agreed, smiling wryly at his own lack of care.

Chloe wasn't the only one experiencing *a first* today. His lapse into physical violence, followed by this reckless plunge into intimacy…he'd never been so beyond normal control that he'd bypassed elementary protection from unwelcome consequences. The feelings she stirred kept pushing him to perform acts above and beyond the usual highly guarded parameters of his life. But now that she'd given herself to him, these aberrations should pass.

Her hand was gently fondling his penis as though she was fascinated with its size and shape and Max felt excitement rising in him again. 'You're playing with fire,' he warned.

'Good!' She lifted her head and threw him a wicked grin. 'I want to watch it grow.'

He laughed, surprised by her uninhibited comment. 'It can't be a mystery to you.'

She cocked her head on one side, eyeing him consideringly. 'I don't think women are a mystery to you, Max, but you wanted to watch me, so why wouldn't I want to watch you?'

Only with her had he felt compelled to see everything she was feeling with him. Whenever he'd had sex with other women he'd simply accepted they were both reaching for mutual satisfaction which invariably eventuated. The extraordinary circumstances had made this more important, he told himself. And the fascinating ability Chloe had to project so much emotion in her eyes, on her beautiful face…how could he not want to see?

'You're a very special woman, Chloe,' he said seriously. 'I didn't want to fail you in any way.'

It turned her serious. 'You don't. All the time you give me what I need, what I want. You never fail. And it's wonderful in one sense…' She paused, frowning slightly.

'But…?' he prompted.

She grimaced. 'It's like I'm being passive in all this and I don't want to be passive anymore.'

His mouth twitched with amusement. 'Believe me. You weren't passive. I wouldn't have completely lost my head if your response had not been so actively exciting.'

She eyed him curiously. 'You don't usually lose your head?'

'No.'

'Does that mean it was especially good for you?'

'Yes.'

She looked enormously pleased, her sky-blue eyes sparkling with joy, her smile so wide the dimples in her cheeks deepened in tantalising provocation and he reached out and placed a teasing finger in one of them. She laughed at his bemusement in her. 'Well, I'm glad I wasn't a failure to you. I would have shrivelled up and died. As it is, I don't feel at all bad about this, even though I should.'

'Why should you?' Surely she couldn't feel guilty about being unfaithful to a marriage that was dead and gone.

She winced. 'In a way, I've just acted like Laura Farrell, though at least you're not married to Shannah Lian.' Her eyes searched his worriedly. 'Did you forget about her, Max?'

It obviously troubled her that he might be in the same unfaithful class as her husband. *She* didn't owe loyalty to anyone, but he…there was empathy for Shannah's situation on her face. 'It's over between Shannah and me,' he quickly assured her. 'We parted friends. You haven't taken anything from her, Chloe. Nor have I cheated on her.'

He watched her process this information. The initial relief gave way to a narrow-eyed re-assessment of her own situation with him. He knew she was thinking of how her mother and husband had interpreted his actions on her behalf, that he was motivated by carnal desire, not keeping his television show on track. There was no more fondling. She drew her hand away from his groin and separated her body from his, sliding to one side, an elbow propping her up as she studied *his* face, her mind obviously whirling with questions.

They were still on an intimate footing, Max told himself. She hadn't flounced off the bed to grab her robe and cover herself. She didn't want to separate herself from him that far. Nevertheless, he knew the next words spoken could have a critical impact on where they went from here. He didn't try to pull her back to him, respecting the space she'd put between them. He didn't move at all but there was a shift inside himself, adrenaline pumping through him, relaxation obliterated by the growing tension of battle readiness.

He wasn't about to lose now.

Chloe decided she wanted the truth, whatever it was. There'd been no gossip about Max breaking up with Shannah Lian, so the break had to be very recent. The big question was *when*? The gorgeous redhead had not been with him at the launch party. Was that an indication the relationship had ended before then…before the revelation of Tony's and Laura's betrayal, which had made her so vulnerable to Max's escape route?

Chloe fiercely hoped so. She didn't want her mother and Tony to be right about Max. He'd been so good to her…good *for* her. On the other hand, she couldn't bear to live with lies. Her whole life felt as though it had been false. Above all, she needed to get it straight now, not be fooled by anything anymore.

There was no guilt in Max's eyes. Not the slightest flicker of evasion, either. He was watching her intently, his dark brilliant gaze very steady and direct, waiting for her to tell him what was on her mind, why she had moved aside, breaking the intimate togetherness. There was waiting in his stillness, too, and the uneasy thought flashed across her mind that it was the stillness of a predator waiting for the right opening to attack.

He'd certainly seized the right opening at the launch party, moving in at the precise moment of absolute vulnerability, taking her into his keeping when she was too shell-shocked to be aware of it. But she wasn't shell-shocked now and she wasn't going to be weak, letting him steam-roll her into an affair that could distract her from what she should be doing.

Another question popped into her mind. She couldn't imagine any woman dumping Max, though it seemed relevant to the main issue so she asked, 'Did you end it or did Shannah?'

'I did.'

No surprise in that admission. Chloe couldn't see Max not being in charge of everything to do with his life. She had to ask the big question now. 'When, Max?'

'The day you came here. I had a dinner date with Shannah that night. I couldn't relate to her. I kept thinking of you.'

Relief swept through her. It sounded reasonable. Yet it didn't really answer the accusations made by her mother and Tony. 'Do you mean wanting me instead of her?'

'Yes.'

She took a deep breath and blurted out, 'Has everything you've done for me been about…about *wanting* me?'

His mouth quirked into an ironic little smile. 'Chloe, I doubt there's a man alive who wouldn't find you desirable, but if you're asking if it was lust driving me to take you into my protection that first night, no, it wasn't.'

A flush of embarrassment burned her cheeks. Of course, it was a ridiculous assumption. He'd whipped her away from a nasty scene because he hadn't wanted the whole focus of the launch party to be diverted into a gossip-fest that had nothing to do with the show.

'I spoke the truth to you,' he quietly assured her. 'Protecting the star of my show, ensuring its success was my top priority. I moved straight into damage control. And I'd have to say I quite enjoyed doing it.'

Going into battle, she thought, not attaching his relish for it to anything personal to her until he added, 'I've always liked you, Chloe. I didn't like the way your mother handled you. I didn't like your husband who was riding on your coat-tails. But that was none of my business until you gave me the go-ahead to act on your behalf to free you from both of them. Only then did I start thinking…she is now free to be with me.'

Having just reasoned away his actions, this statement came as a shock. Chloe didn't know what to think of it and Max moved, startling her into rolling onto her back as he propped himself on his side, his eyes glittering with dark, ruthless purpose, his hand reaching out to cup her cheek and keep her attention fixed on him.

'I wanted that, Chloe. I wanted that immediately. And proceeded to do everything possible to make it happen. For you to be with me,' he said without the slightest hint of apology. 'But it could only happen if you wanted it, too. If you chose to be with me.'

Choices…yes. All along he had presented her with choices; tempting choices, seductive choices, reasonable choices, everything possible that would appeal to her state of mind. And heart. She couldn't call it a trap when she had walked into it willingly. Even though she had sensed that her white knight had a dark side, it hadn't stopped her going with him, wanting to be with him.

He hadn't interfered with her marriage. Tony had done that, not Max.

He hadn't *taken her over*, as her mother had put it, colouring him with her own *using* mentality.

Yes, he had dumped Shannah Lian for her, and Chloe was glad she was the more desirable woman to him and he had been honest about it, acting honourably, ending one relationship before pursuing another.

He had done nothing wrong.

And everything right for her.

What more could she ask of him?

The frantic pumping of her heart eased.

He smiled, as though he knew the cloud of troubling concerns had lifted from her mind. 'I think I'm good for you. Tell me if I'm not.'

The last of her inner tension dissolved in a gurgle of laughter. He was a beautiful man—an infinitely desirable man and she was enormously fortunate that he desired her. She raised her hands to cup his wickedly handsome face, smiling as she drew it down towards hers. 'I like how good you are for me, Max.'

He laughed, his eyes twinkling delight in her response. Their kiss started with a sense of mutual joy in each other but quickly escalated into passion. Excitement fizzed through her body, re-energising it into a wild craving for more intimacy with him. He was ready for it, too. She reached down and stroked him, marvelling again at how hard and powerful he felt, elated that she stirred such strong desire in this marvellous man.

'No more feeling passive,' he murmured against her lips, then lifted her to sit astride him as he rolled onto his back, grinning a wicked invitation as he said, 'Take me.'

She did, loving the sensation of slowly sinking down on him, feeling him filling her inside. Her grin back at him was pure blissful pleasure. He reached up and started caressing her breasts, his thumbs teasing her nipples, his dark eyes simmering a challenge for her to be as active as she liked. Chloe had never thought of herself as an exhibitionist, yet she revelled in rolling her hips, swaying her body in an intensely sensual and tantalising rhythm, watching him watching her, seeing the simmer in his eyes flare into a blaze of urgent need.

He whipped her onto her back, seizing control, plunging fast and furiously, driving her excitement to the same shattering peak as before, both of them crying out as they climaxed together, both of them subsiding into a languorous state of sweet satiation afterwards. Chloe lay in his embrace, savouring a sense of perfect happiness. She didn't care if it was only ever going to be a temporary thing with Max. It was good. Better than anything she'd known in her entire life.

A questioning whine from the bedroom doorway snapped her head up from Max's chest. Luther! He was standing quite normally on his sturdy little legs, his eyes bright, his head cocked to one side, observing the fact there were two people on the bed instead of one and looking not too sure that he wouldn't get kicked again.

'It's okay, Luther,' Chloe promised him. 'See—' Max obligingly raised his head '—it's Max.'

'Come on, little fella. Want to join us?' Max crooned at him, throwing out a welcoming arm.

Luther happily scampered over to the bed and Max gently scooped him onto it, whereupon the little dog darted from one to the other, licking their faces in exuberant pleasure that all was well in their world. Clearly he'd suffered no damage from Tony's kick, and they finally settled him down between them, stroking him into blissful contentment.

'I'm glad I gave him to you,' Max said in a fond tone. 'If he hadn't been barking his head off this afternoon, alerting me to trouble, I'd still be wondering how long I'd have to wait before you felt comfortable about admitting the attraction between us.'

She sighed over the needless tension she'd put herself through. 'I thought I kept it hidden from you.'

He shook his head. 'You can't hide sexual chemistry,

Chloe, and it's always been there between us. It was why you never felt comfortable in my presence. You clung to your mother or Tony, using them as safety barriers because you didn't feel safe with me.'

His perception shamed her in a way because she hadn't faced up to the truth in the past, her mind instinctively shying away from examining the feelings he stirred in her, labeling him dangerous—to be avoided whenever possible, kept at a distance when he was unavoidable. 'Well, I feel safe with you now,' she said decisively.

Although she wasn't safe from falling in love with him.

And he would move on from her, just as he'd moved on from Shannah Lian. That was his well-documented reputation with women, as her mother had pointed out. She couldn't expect it to turn out differently with her. She still had to keep Max at a distance…from her heart.

He frowned at her. 'What are you thinking?'

'I'm thinking I'll take all you want to give me of yourself for as long as you want me with you, but I mustn't get too addicted to it because it will come to an end sooner or later.'

Max instantly thought, *I might not want it to come to an end*, but he pulled himself back from saying it. He'd never held out even the suggestion of a lasting relationship to any woman and it would be wrong to plant the idea of it Chloe's mind. He didn't know the future. He knew this woman was different to the others who'd passed through his life, knew she evoked feelings that were not usually touched in him, but this was all very new and it was happening now. Next month…next year…sooner or later…the feelings might wane.

'All I want to give you of myself,' he repeated musingly,

his eyes teasing hers. 'That's a sweeping statement, Chloe. You might want to draw limits. You can, you know. You're free to make whatever choices you like. I don't own you. I hope you won't ever let anyone own you again.'

It was good advice and he saw it sink in, saw her shedding the kind of ownership her mother and husband had inflicted on her, saw the realisation that her life was hers to shape any way she liked, saw the will to do it being born, saw her slipping away from him.

Which gave him the weird sense that he'd just cut his own throat and might end up bleeding to death from caring about her too much.

But it was still good advice and he wouldn't take it back.

He didn't want to be selfish with her.

She deserved to flower into the person she could be, freed from the suppression of her past life. He would enjoy watching her become that person—a survivor like him, moving forward, finding her own sunshine, opening up to it, seizing the opportunities that appealed to her. The husk of her mother's Chloe would be left behind and the Maria in her mind would emerge.

Maria…

Mary…

CHAPTER ELEVEN

CHLOE did set limits. She would not go out in public with Max. First, it was bound to create a frenzy of gossip, bringing the paparazzi down on her like a cloud of bees, just when they'd lost interest since nothing juicy had eventuated from her move to Max's guest house. Second, the cast of the show would inevitably treat her differently. She'd already had a taste of that and decided that it would be much easier working with them if their suspicions about her relationship with Max were not confirmed. Third, she didn't want to give Tony any nasty ammunition to fire at her, nor give her mother the smug satisfaction that once again she'd known better than Chloe. Which she hadn't, but she'd think it.

'When we've finished shooting this season's episodes for the show, and I've moved to a place of my own, then I'll go out with you if you still want me to,' she'd said, being very firm on this point.

'Uh-huh,' Max had agreed, a gleam of wry amusement in his eyes. 'I can see that making an independent stand is important to you. But in the meantime, can we carry on in private?'

She'd laughed and hugged him. 'I'd be very disappointed if we didn't.'

'Then I shall attempt to make what time we have together as entertaining as I can.'

He did. For Chloe it was almost an idyllic existence, living in the children's house and being with Max. There were so many pleasures—making love, watching episodes of *M*A*S*H* together, sailing, lazing by the pool, sharing the delicious dinners Elaine cooked for them in the big house, watching and discussing television shows Max was interested in acquiring.

At first she'd been a bit self-conscious about their new relationship where the three E's were concerned, but she needn't have worried about their reaction to it. Edgar maintained his air of deference at all times. Elaine, who was an avid fan of the show and loved how Chloe played her part in it, was only too happy to have a closer acquaintance with her and always welcomed Luther into her kitchen. Eric seemed to assume she was becoming a fixture at Hill House and took to asking her opinion of whatever he'd been doing around the grounds.

It would have been so easy to let everything else slide. Happiness was addictive. But the sense that she had to get her own life in order—apart from Max—could not be ignored. That had been her worst mistake in the past, letting things slide. She would not be guilty of it again.

Max gave her the name of a good divorce lawyer, whom she met, subsequently setting the ultimate separation from Tony in motion, listening very carefully to the legal issues involved so she could fully understand her position and make sensible decisions. The lawyer assured her he would negotiate a fair settlement with Tony, not allowing her husband to milk the divorce for more than he was entitled to.

She bought herself a little car, a white VW Beetle, which was cute and comfortable and easy to park in the city. Having acquired her own transport, as well as the confidence to handle her own problems, she dispensed with Gerry Anderson's services, thanking the security guard for having taken such good care of her and Luther.

'A pleasure, Miss Rollins. You have my card. Call me if you ever have a problem I can help you with,' he'd said with a touching sincerity, which left Chloe feeling she had a ready friend if she ever required a security guard again.

She needed the car in her hunt for suitable accommodation. Her choice was limited because most apartment complexes would not allow pets and no way was she going to part with Luther. She didn't want to commit herself to buying a property, not before her divorce was settled, so finding something right to rent was difficult. Saturday mornings were taken up with looking at places, none of which really fitted her requirements.

'I'd like something close to a park that I can take Luther to,' she remarked to Max after being disappointed in her search once again.

'There's no time pressure, Chloe. I'm perfectly happy for you to stay on here beyond the two months,' he assured her.

She gave him an arch look. 'I don't intend to hang on until it doesn't suit you, Max.'

He frowned. 'I wasn't suggesting you do.' The dark brilliant eyes sharply probed hers. 'I like what we have together, Chloe. It may suit me for a very long time.'

Her heart skipped a beat. She liked it, too. She loved it. But indulging in forever dreams with Max was not good for her. A long time might only mean a year or two.

Max watched the temptation to stay with him slip into uncertainty and the urge to do battle with her doubts was too insistent to deny. He liked coming home to her, more than he could ever have imagined coming home to anyone. He felt a buzz of joyful anticipation each time he drove through the gateway and it wasn't so much the welcoming sight of Hill House he looked forward to, but being with Chloe again. She delighted him in every sense.

'You're happy here,' he argued. 'Luther is happy here. Eric and Elaine are happy to mind him when you go out. When *we* go out. As we will as soon as your work on this season's episodes is done.'

They were in the children's house and he drew her into his embrace, deliberately reminding her of the ready intimacy they shared. He stroked her cheek as his eyes bored into hers, commanding her surrender to his will. 'You love this place,' he said with soft seductive persuasion. 'You have your own car, your independence. You can pay me rent if that will make you feel more right about staying on.' He moved his fingers to her lips, arousing sensitivity to his touch. 'I want you to stay, Chloe.'

He saw a multitude of emotions warring in her eyes—desire, hope, yearning, fear, panic…the latter jolting his drive to win what he wanted.

She pushed away from him, words tumbling out in a desperate burst. 'I can't, Max. I can't. Don't ask me to.'

Her hands clapped her cheeks, smacking off the lingering influence of his touch. Her eyes begged him to understand. Max didn't but he stood still, instinctively knowing he had to wait for her to explain, not press for anything. It appalled him that he had struck fear in her. She was precious to him. Hurting her in any shape or form had never been his intention.

Her hands dropped from her face. She wrung them as she gulped in deep breaths, struggling for control of the agitation that had gripped her. Max was acutely aware of feeling more tension than he did in any critical business meeting. He'd always been prepared for them, confident of coming out on top, but he'd had no experience of what was happening here and now with Chloe.

She gathered herself to speak. 'All my life…' She stopped, swallowed hard, started again. 'For most of my life, I did what my mother wanted. I learned…she made me learn…it was easier to obey, easier not to resist, easier just to fall in with whatever she decided.'

Max saw the memories of punishment flit through her eyes and his jaw clenched at a surge of hatred for Stephanie Rollins. He'd been the victim of negligence, indifference, crazy outbursts of emotion from his own mother throughout his boyhood, but never cruelly pressured into performing to her will.

'Then when I married Tony and realised I was only a tool to him, too…someone he could use to get what he wanted…I took the easy path again, letting him do it because at least he made the process more pleasant than my mother did. He pretended to love me. I could live with that. He made it easy.'

The con man keeping his gravy train sweet, Max thought in blistering contempt. Yet a disturbing niggle of conscience started whispering he was doing a very similar thing.

'And it would be all too easy for me to stay on here with you, Max,' Chloe went on, nailing the tack he had used to keep her with him. 'But if I did that, I'd be slipping back into the same old pattern that I need to break, giving you control of my life instead of being in charge of it myself.'

'No!' he vehemently denied. 'I would not control your life, Chloe. You'd always have freedom of choice with me.'

Pained eyes looked back at him. 'I can't choose when

you'll meet some other woman who sparks your interest, Max. Shannah Lian had no choice at all in the end, did she?'

But it's different with you.

The words burned to be said. He barely stopped them from exploding off his tongue. As true as it was, it didn't promise the kind of longevity that would mean they would never part. They were still in the honeymoon phase of their relationship. The deeply honed pragmatic part of his mind dictated a much longer period was required to test the depth of his feelings for her. Rushing into some rash declaration would not serve either of them well.

'I need a place of my own, Max,' she asserted with quiet conviction, her eyes pleading for his acceptance. No more argument. 'I don't ever want to feel again I have nowhere to go if…other things…start falling apart.' Her lips quivered into a wry little smile. 'It might not be so convenient for you…for either of us…'

'That's not important.' His hand sliced the air in sharp dismissal. 'Your sense of well-being is. I'm sorry. I wasn't thinking…just wanting to hold onto what we've been sharing.' He shook his head in mute apology as he moved to reassure her, his hands curling gently around her shoulders, his eyes projecting empathy with her feelings. 'When my mother died, the welfare people moved me to a hostel. I couldn't wait to leave school, earn enough money to get a place of my own. Do you want me to help you find one, Chloe?'

Relief and joy sparkled back at him as she wound her arms around his waist, pressing close to him. 'No. You've helped me enough, Max. I can't tell you how much I appreciate all you've done for me. Even when we're not lovers anymore, I'll always consider you the best friend I could ever have had.'

'Hmmm... I'm not ready to end the lovers part yet. Are you?'

'No.' She looked wickedly at him as she rubbed her lower body against his.

He laughed and scooped her up in his arms, needing to assuage the strong sense of possessiveness that he had to contain. Luther barked at the exuberant action and he smiled down at the dog. 'You get your fair share of her, little fella. This is my turn.'

Chloe laughed as he strode to the bedroom and kicked the door shut behind them. There was no sense of conflict between them as they made love. Chloe gave herself to him with uninhibited pleasure and Max revelled in the certainty that she would still be his woman, regardless of a change in residence.

Lying together afterwards, he felt a deep tenderness towards her, cuddling her close, softly stroking her hair and the lovely curve of her spine. 'You are safe with me, Chloe,' he murmured. 'I'm not out to exploit you in any way.'

She sighed, her breath drifting warmly across his chest. 'I know that, Max. You don't need to. You run your own race.'

Which she had not done up until now. He understood her need to take control, given the victimisation she had helplessly resigned herself to in the past. It was right for her to establish her own ground, her own space. Yet the simple truth she had just spoken made him think about the life he had made for himself—running his own race.

He'd had to as a child. His mother had been totally irresponsible. More times than not there was no food bought for him, her single mother's pension all spent on drugs. She'd slept in most mornings, not worrying about getting him off to school. He went because it was better than staying with her, trying to shut off her rants about whatever got stuck in her mind.

It had been a lonely life, looking after himself. Becoming self-sufficient had not been an easy journey but it had been the only way to survive in his mother's environment. He'd hated it when she had bursts of sentimentality, hugging him, rocking him in an excess of emotion as she raved on about how much she loved her little boy. Her so-called love was just some mushy thing that had no reality attached to it. Max remembered thinking he would be much better off without it.

And he had done very well without it—running his own race—not letting anything or anyone divert him from achieving the goals he set for himself.

But would he be content to keep it that way, having spent this brilliant time with Chloe, sharing more with her than he had with any other person—man or woman—enjoying everything about her? He'd never minded being alone. It had been an advantage, not having consideration for other people hold him back from what he chose to do. He'd consciously avoided emotional strings that might tie him down. Yet he knew he would miss Chloe's ready company when he came home.

He couldn't stop this private idyll from coming to an end. However, he didn't have to accept an uncrossable distance between them. The need to nail down some definite future with her was paramount. There was so much more he wanted to share with her, introduce her to.

'When you leave here, Chloe, keeping our relationship a secret will become untenable,' he said matter-of-factly. 'Someone will pick up on my visiting you. You will want me to visit, won't you?' he added confidently.

'Yes, of course,' she said without hesitation.

'Then I see no reason why we shouldn't appear in public together. Work on the show will have finished for the season.

By the time we start the next set of episodes, the cast and crew will be used to the fact that we've linked up so our relationship will be taken for granted, not be a hot item for speculation. It shouldn't cause you any discomfort. Agreed?'

She didn't answer.

Max felt tension seizing him again as he waited. He couldn't force her to agree with him. She had to want to. He couldn't see her face, didn't know what was going through her mind. Her marriage was dead. She shouldn't be worrying about what Tony thought. Or what her mother thought. She now had her own life to do whatever she liked with it. Surely she would choose to spend as much time with him as they could arrange. No way would he accept remaining her secret lover! It was too limited!

Chloe's mind was in turmoil. It was a daunting prospect, being publicly linked to such a powerful man, being labelled his new paramour, which would inevitably raise speculation on how long this liaison would last, given Max's reputation for moving on. On top of that, despite the lapse of time since her separation from Tony, her relationship with Max could still be viewed as scandalous. The paparazzi would be all over every appearance they made together.

She shrank from having to face it, wishing they could still be lovers in private. These past two months had been heaven, so easy…

Easy.

The word mocked her, instantly accusing her of sliding back into her old mindset. She'd just made a stand with Max over not taking the easy path of staying with him here. Not only that, at the beginning of their affair, she'd insisted they not appear in public together until the show was wrapped up for this season and she had a place of her own. As he'd just pointed out, that time was almost up. Backtracking on her word, denying him what he wanted when he'd given her so much was simply not on. Besides, she knew she would crave his companionship, in every sense.

So what if it wasn't easy going public!

She'd have Max at her side.

That was more important to her than anything else.

Having him.

She lifted herself up from his chest to smile that assurance at him. 'I will be very pleased to go out with you, Max,' she said, secretly wanting far more from him than she could ever ask or expect—like having this amazingly wonderful man with her for the rest of her life.

'Good!' A smile of satisfaction spread across his face.

Chloe told herself to be satisfied, too. The experience of Max had already changed her life for the better. She would always be grateful he had stepped into it...even when he stepped out of it.

CHAPTER TWELVE

ON the Saturday before the last week of shooting the show, Chloe finally found a place she was happy to rent. It was a small terrace house, situated on a street that ran parallel to Centennial Park. She didn't care that it was old and in need of some modernisation in the kitchen and bathroom. It was functional—two bedrooms upstairs, enough living space downstairs, with a small, enclosed backyard so that Luther didn't have to be kept inside all the time—and being right across the street from the park was ideal. It was also close to the shops she knew from living at Randwick.

It was a huge emotional wrench, leaving the children's house, saying goodbye to the three E's, who had contributed so much to her comfort while she was staying there, moving away from the daily intimacy with Max. She was glad to have Luther's company, staving off the loneliness she might have felt, though she occupied herself very busily during the first week after the move, arranging her belongings in her new accommodation, acquiring the furniture she needed, having a dog door inserted into the door to the backyard and teaching Luther how to use it.

Max dropped by most evenings to see how she was getting

on, bringing her flowers and gourmet treats from Elaine's kitchen. They invariably ended up in bed together, which was the best treat of all to Chloe. He only had to look at her and her whole body started buzzing with anticipation for the sexual connection between them.

Sometimes they didn't make it upstairs to the bedroom. Like when he brought her a bunch of the most gloriously scented yellow roses and he took the one she'd held up to her nose and caressed her skin with it; her cheeks, her neck, down the V-neckline of her shirt, undoing the buttons, brushing it over the swell of her breasts...he'd hoisted her up on the kitchen bench and had incredibly erotic and exciting sex with her there.

He was a fantastic lover. Chloe had a losing battle on her hands, fighting to keep him at any distance from her heart. He made her feel so beautifully loved, so wonderfully cared for. Had he treated all the women in his life like this, or was she more special than the others? He'd said she was special. The tantalising question was *how* special? Enough to want her with him for the rest of their lives?

They started going out together. They went to parties, to charity functions, to the theatre, ballet, opera, walked the red carpet together at a film premiere. They were the talk of the town—the television baron coupled with the star of his latest hit show. Max handled the red-hot interest with practised ease. Chloe simply glowed her pleasure in his company. It wasn't difficult. She loved being with him and didn't care what anyone else thought.

However she did refuse one request from him, that she hostess a dinner party at Hill House. Somehow that was too much like being a pseudo-wife. Fulfilling that role was too close to her secret yearning to be his lifetime partner. She wouldn't let herself pretend. She was finished with pretence.

In fact, she shied away from returning to Hill House at all, knowing it would tug at her heart, make her wish it was her home. It had been hard enough to leave. She didn't want to feel that wrench over and over again.

Max grew frustrated by her turning down his invitations to join him there. 'You liked Hill House. You liked the three E's. They liked you. They miss you, Chloe,' he argued.

He didn't say *he* missed her. Max wasn't into revealing any weakness in himself. There were no cracks in his self-contained armour. She had to learn to be self-contained, too. 'It's *your* home, Max. I don't belong there,' she quietly asserted.

He frowned. 'You don't have to belong. What's wrong with visiting?'

She shook her head. 'I can't go back. I have to move on in my own way. You see me as much as you like, don't you? We go out a lot together. Doesn't that satisfy what you want from me in our relationship?'

He stared at the appeal in her eyes for long, nerve-tearing moments. 'Your choice,' he finally said with a grimace that seemed to mock himself.

Much to Chloe's relief, he didn't raise the issue again. He arranged dinner parties at restaurants. She didn't mind being his partner on these occasions. It was not the same as being his hostess at Hill House.

The rest period before shooting the next set of episodes for the show was almost up when Chloe received an unexpected and highly unwelcome visitor at her terrace house. It was a Monday morning and she'd just done a load of washing and was about to have a coffee break when the doorbell rang.

Luther raced down the hallway, barking at the noise. Probably a delivery person, Chloe thought—Max sending flowers. Nevertheless, she took the precaution of looking through the peephole in the door to check.

Her heart instantly contracted with shock.

Laura Farrell was on her front porch. She was standing side-on, the baby bump clearly visible, outlined by the form-fitting grey skirt and grey-and-white top she wore. Her long brown hair fell lankly forward, hiding much of her face. Her shoulders drooped. As Chloe was still coming to terms with the identity of her visitor, Laura turned, reaching out to press the doorbell again, her face devoid of make-up and her amber eyes leaking tears.

Chloe jerked back from the peephole, her mind reeling with confusion as well as shock. Why would a weeping Laura Farrell come to her doorstep? She couldn't possibly hope to be rehired as a personal assistant after such a flagrant betrayal of trust and the vicious verbal attack at the launch party. What on earth did she expect to gain by coming here? Forgive and forget?

Not in a million years, Chloe thought as the doorbell kept ringing, sending the message that Laura Farrell was not about to give up and go away. While part of her inwardly recoiled from facing the woman again, another part insisted on putting a decisive end to whatever was on Laura's mind—affirmative action. She was no longer the old Chloe who had been brain-washed into avoiding any form of confrontation. She'd learnt how to handle a lot of things since being with Max.

Luther was barking his head off. She bent and scooped him up in her arms to calm him down, then opened the door, in-tending to tell Laura she was not welcome in her home.

'Thank God you're here!' Laura cried in pathetic relief, her hands jerking into a trembling gesture of appeal. 'Please, Chloe, I have to talk to you. I have no-one else to turn to. Tony…' She broke into sobs, covering her face with her hands, shaking her head in anguish.

Chloe didn't want to be moved by the other woman's distress. What happened between Laura and Tony was their business, not hers, and she certainly didn't want to be involved in it. Yet it seemed too cruel and callous to send her away in this state.

'You'd better come in,' she said reluctantly, standing back to give her entry.

'Oh, thank you, thank you,' Laura babbled brokenly.

Luther barked at her as she stumbled into the hallway, instinctively picking up Chloe's dislike of the situation. He started to wriggle in her arms, wanting to get down and check out this visitor to his satisfaction, but Chloe held onto him until she saw Laura seated at the dining table and fetched a box of tissues for her to mop up the tears.

'Would you like a cup of tea?' she asked, knowing it was Laura's preferred drink.

A nod as she snuffled into a tissue.

'I'm letting my dog go now. He's sure to sniff around your feet. I'd advise you not to kick him,' she warned.

'Wouldn't do that,' Laura choked out.

Chloe released Luther, who instantly did as expected. Leaving the little terrier on guard duty, she went to the kitchen, made Laura a cup of tea and herself a coffee, and took them to the dining table. She sat across the table from her ex-personal assistant, who had assisted herself to her employer's husband, waiting for her to be composed enough to speak.

Laura finally raised a woebegone face and in a despairing

voice, said, 'Tony has abandoned me. Even though I'm having his baby, he won't give me any support.'

Chloe was shocked to hear this. Despite his lies and infidelity and the nasty burst of temper that had lashed out at Luther, she hadn't thought him a complete and utter rotter.

'I can't get another job. No-one wants a pregnant P.A.,' Laura wailed. 'I need help, Chloe. I can't manage having a baby without help.'

Lots of single mothers had to manage by themselves, Chloe thought, and Laura was definitely not a helpless kind of person, but maybe she was floundering in a trough of depression and couldn't see a way forward. 'Do you want me to speak to Tony about this?' she asked, thinking Laura had one hell of a hide to want that from the injured wife.

She shook her head. 'It's useless. He's furious that I told you, won't have anything to do with me. Or the baby.' Tears welled again. 'I'm sorry I told you the way I did, Chloe, but I was so upset, so madly in love with him, I was out of my mind that night. He was my baby's father and all I could think of was he had to break from you and marry me.'

Despite the offence to herself, Chloe couldn't help feeling a little tug of sympathy. The baby did make a difference. Although Laura shouldn't have been having an affair with Tony in the first place.

And she knew it, immediately trying to justify it, her whole body leaning forward in an appeal for understanding as she rattled on. 'I tried not to fall in love with him. He was your husband and on every moral ground he was out of bounds to me. I truly struggled against the attraction I felt, Chloe, but he sensed it and played on it. I liked working for you. I didn't want to give up my job, but I was terribly drawn to Tony and one night when I'd had too much to drink, he seduced me into bed with him. I'm as much a victim of his charming ways as you are. I thought he really did love me and his marriage to you was just a sham to further his career. I'm terribly sorry you were hurt but at least now you've got Max Hart so you've moved on and up.'

'I've certainly moved on but divorce brings everyone down and having Max as a friend does not mean I'm up,' she sharply corrected her.

'More than a friend surely,' she snapped back, an envious flash in her eyes.

Better value than Tony.

She didn't say it but Chloe knew she was thinking it, and instantly started bridling against the mercenary aspect of Laura's outlook. She cut to the chase.

'Why have you come here, Laura?'

She gave an anguished shake of her head. Her hands fluttered in agitation. 'I'm out of work. I thought Tony would support me but he won't and I can't pay the rent on my apartment. I'm almost destitute, Chloe.' Her eyes begged for help. 'I don't have anyone to turn to. We used to be friends. If I hadn't been thrown so much into Tony's company because of working for you…'

Anger stirred. 'Are you saying your pregnancy is my fault?'

'No…no…but he did deceive both of us. I thought you might understand and forgive how it was, and for the sake of the baby…please, Chloe…if you could lend me some money to tide me over for a while…just bypass Tony and give me what he should be giving me. You could tell your lawyer what it's for and he could deduct it out of Tony's divorce settlement.'

The cash cow… Chloe couldn't forget that phrase. She

wanted no part of this—none at all. Yet there was an innocent baby involved and she was appalled at Tony's callous dismissal of it. 'What sum of money do you have in mind?' she asked, careful not to commit herself to anything.

Triumph…greed…something glittered in the amber eyes that was at odds with Laura's supposed desperation, although the glitter was quickly swallowed up by another gush of tears. 'I hate asking this of you…' She blotted up the moisture with a tissue, blinked rapidly, took a deep breath and gabbled, 'Maybe a lump sum settlement would be best. I could go away, make a life for my child somewhere else, a more simple existence…'

'How much, Laura?' Chloe bored in, hating this scene.

She wrung her hands, looked distracted, then hesitantly, pleadingly answered, 'If you could write me a cheque for fifty thousand dollars…'

Fifty thousand!

The sheer boldness of it floored Chloe for a moment. Had she been such a walkover person in the past? Apply emotional pressure and she'd buckle to it every time? No mind of her own? Is that what Laura had been counting on?

However, there was still the baby to be considered.

'I won't hand out that amount of money, Laura,' she said decisively. 'I *will* talk to my lawyer about your situation and get him to talk to Tony's lawyer….'

'But that could take weeks…months…I'm down to the dregs of my bank account now,' she wailed.

'I assure you something will be done to persuade Tony into shouldering his responsibility within days,' Chloe said with steely resolve, rising from the dining table to put an end to the distasteful conversation.

'He won't…he won't,' she cried, remaining seated and burying her face in her hands.

Luther, who'd also sprung to his feet as Chloe had risen to hers, started barking at her to get up, too. Laura ignored him. Chloe sighed impatiently, shushed Luther and spoke very firmly, 'I promise you, something will be done about getting child support to you one way or another. There's no more to be said, Laura.'

'Oh, please, Chloe…' She stumbled up from her chair—a picture of wretched despair. 'Don't send me away with nothing. I don't know what I'll do.'

Was that a threat of suicide?

Luther started barking again, not liking whatever his instincts were picking up.

'If you could just give me a cheque for five thousand,' Laura begged.

Chloe didn't like it but she was troubled enough to go to her handbag and extract five hundred dollars from her purse. She held out the notes to Laura. 'That's all I have on hand. It should help enough until other money comes through for you.'

She took the money, though still pressing for more. 'I could cash a cheque…'

'No. I've promised to act on your behalf and I'll keep my word. That's it, Laura. I want you to leave now.'

Chloe headed off down the hallway to open the front door. Luther stayed behind to bark at Laura until she followed. Which she did, weeping so noisily, Chloe felt it was a deliberate attempt to weaken her resolve. Though it might not be. She hated this. It was churning her up, making it difficult to cling to her sense of rightness in how she had acted.

Laura paused in the doorway to start pleading pitifully again.

'No, stop!' Chloe cried, completely out of patience. 'Don't come here again, Laura. I won't be swayed into doing any more for you.'

Amazingly, her screwed-up face suddenly smoothed out. The leaking eyes flashed fury. She lashed out, not the slightest wobble in her voice. 'What are a few measly thousands to you when you're feathering your nest with Max Hart's billions? Next to nothing!' The vicious tone turned into wheedling. 'This is so bad of you, Chloe, sending me off with a pittance, not caring about the baby...'

Luther growled and jumped at Laura's legs, making her scuttle onto the porch away from him. Chloe immediately shut the door and locked it, breathing a grateful sigh of relief. She bent and scooped the little terrier up in her arms. 'Good dog, saving me again,' she crooned, petting him lovingly as she headed for the backyard, wanting as much distance as possible between her and Laura Farrell.

Her head was throbbing and her insides felt all twisted up. So many times in the past she had given in to whatever was being demanded of her, needing to end this awful inner turmoil, but she didn't feel bad about not giving in to Laura. This was Tony's fault, not hers. Tony's responsibility. Laura's, too. It was wrong that *she* should be expected to fix the situation.

Although she would call her lawyer and set up a meeting with Tony. One way or another, he had to be made to give his child appropriate support.

Max parked his Audi outside Chloe's terrace house at Centennial Park and wished once again she was still living with him at Vaucluse. He'd liked having her on hand, liked the sense of going home to her. He knew it was important to her to be independent of him, knew he should be pleased about it for her sake, but it didn't please him.

It pleased him even less when he went inside and listened to her account of Laura Farrell's visit and the outcome of it with Chloe involving herself with Tony Lipton again. It was pointless telling her she shouldn't have given any money to Laura. The baby was the big issue with Chloe. Max suspected it was always going to be a big issue—one that would inevitably separate them if he didn't rethink his life.

'Anyhow, I told my lawyer I wanted urgent action on this and he's set up a meeting with Tony in his office tomorrow,' she finished with a grimace of distaste. 'It's going to be horrid but I can't just forget it, Max.'

'No,' he agreed. 'It will play on your mind until it's settled. But don't assume Laura told you the truth, Chloe. There's something very fishy about her story.'

Like a lot of emotional pressure for the big handout—a very clever piece of manipulation that Chloe might have fallen for a few months ago, the kind of manipulation Laura would undoubtedly have seen used on Chloe by both Stephanie Rollins and Tony.

She laughed. 'Luther didn't like the smell of it, either.'

Max smiled. 'I made a good choice, getting him for you. Worth his weight in gold.'

'Absolutely!' She wound her arms around his neck, her lovely face tilted up to his, eyes shining pleasure in his gift. 'You have a happy knack of getting everything right, Max.'

He slid his arms around her waist, drawing her closer. 'Would you like me to go with you tomorrow? Help sort things out with Tony?'

'No. This is something I should do myself.' Her mouth curled into an ironic smile. 'I can't expect you to protect me forever.'

The urge to do precisely that was very strong. Max found it difficult to back off from it. Probably his intense dislike of her ex-husband was driving it. He didn't want Chloe meeting with the slime. Yet the encounter with Laura Farrell had definitely demonstrated she could no longer be influenced into doing anything she didn't feel was right. She was no-one's fool anymore, and he had no right to fray her confidence in handling a situation which she saw as her business.

'Besides, I should be perfectly safe in my lawyer's office,' she insisted.

'True,' he conceded. 'I'm worried about when you leave it. If Tony turns nasty…' No mental strength could fight superior physical strength. Chloe *needed* him to protect her.

She frowned, fretting over the very real possibility that Tony could try physical force on her until a solution struck. 'I know. I'll call Gerry Anderson, ask him to take me to the lawyer's office and bring me home. Gerry's a very good security guard.'

An independent solution.

Little by little she was separating herself from him.

Soon she wouldn't need him at all, although wanting him was still strong. He made sure it would stay strong, pouring every bit of his sexual expertise into their love-making later in the evening. Afterwards she cuddled up to him with a satisfied sigh and murmured, 'You know, Max, I'm not with you because I want to feather my nest with your billions. You don't think that, do you?'

'No, I don't. Never would with you, Chloe.'

She snuggled down contentedly, accepting his word without question.

Max knew he couldn't buy her.

Wouldn't want to, either.

Her heart and mind were now geared to making the choices that felt right to her—running her own race.

To keep her he had to make himself *her* choice.

The hell of it was he wanted her to share everything with him, wanted to share everything with her. Running his own race into the future looked very empty without her at his side. Even Hill House felt empty without her there to come home to.

Max had never thought of his life as dark. A deep sense of purpose had driven it forward from nothing to everything he wanted. But Chloe lit him up inside with her lovely, shining, artless personality and all he had valued in the past—the brilliance of his achievements—lost its gloss compared to what she made him feel.

The plain truth was he didn't have everything he wanted.

Chloe was slipping away from him and he wanted more of her.

CHAPTER THIRTEEN

DESPITE Chloe's determination to set things right, she felt very nervous about the confrontation with Tony. He was sure to be angry and spiteful, and although their respective lawyers would be at the meeting—hopefully keeping the situation calm and orderly—having to face her husband again was not a pleasant prospect.

'I can feel your tension, Miss Rollins,' Gerry Anderson remarked caringly as they set out on the drive into the city. 'Want to spell out the problem so I'll know what to watch out for?'

He was a nice man. She had always felt comfortable with him. It was easy to tell him what had happened with Laura Farrell and the purpose of this meeting with her husband.

'May I give you a piece of advice?' he said when she'd finished.

'Please do.'

'Miss Farrell was using every angle she could to milk you. Sounds like a very practised con lady to me and I've had a lot of experience with that kind of person. Don't be surprised if she's already milked Mr Lipton for all she could get.'

'You mean she lied to me about Tony not giving her anything?' It was a stunning thought.

'I'm just saying it's a possibility. For my money, she was going after the cream with you.' He shot her a smile of approval. 'I'm glad you didn't fall for it.'

Chloe grimaced. 'I did give her five hundred dollars.'

'Not too bad a loss. And it made you feel better, which was fair enough. I think you'll probably have to accept it as a loss. I doubt you'll get it back from Mr Lipton. In fact, I think you should listen carefully to his side of the situation before accusing him of anything.' He glanced a quick appeal at her. 'Okay?'

'Yes. Thank you, Gerry,' she said thoughtfully. 'I really appreciate your advice.'

He smiled and nodded. 'Glad to be of assistance to you, Miss Rollins.'

'I'm glad I called you. I feel more…more prepared now.'

'I'll be right on hand if you run into any trouble,' he assured her.

'Thank you,' she said on a sigh of relief.

Having parked the car under the Opera House, Gerry escorted her up Castlereigh Street to her lawyer's chambers and settled himself in the legal secretary's office, right outside the door to the boardroom where the meeting was to be held. Tony and his lawyer were already there when hers walked her in.

The men were dressed in sober dark grey suits. She'd also worn a suit—a light pink linen—and after the preliminary formal greetings, Tony complimented her on it, smiling at her as though he was delighted to be in her company again.

'You look lovely, Chloe,' he said, throwing her into confusion with his charming manner.

She looked at the lawyers in agitated appeal. 'Let's get down to business, shall we?'

They sat at a long boardroom table, each party on opposite sides.

Tony leaned forward, hands outstretched in appeal as he earnestly stated, 'Laura lied to you, Chloe. She lied to me. She's not pregnant. Never was. It was all a lie.'

She'd been prepared for lies but not this. Nothing like this. Her mind reeled with shock. 'But…but I saw her. She had a baby bump. Four or five months…'

'Clever padding, I promise you,' Tony asserted. 'When the other guy she'd tricked contacted me, I insisted that Laura accompany me to a doctor to have the pregnancy confirmed. She wouldn't do it, carrying on about me not trusting her, trying to get me to back off from having proof of pregnancy. No way. She's done this before. Blackmail and fraud.'

Chloe stared at him, barely able to take in what he was saying. She kept seeing Laura standing on her front porch in profile, her pregnancy on obvious show. Was Tony spinning a story to suit himself?

'What other guy?' she asked, finally homing in on his back-up proof for the accusation of blackmail and fraud.

'He'd read the story about our break-up in the newspapers. Laura Farrell's part in it. He thought about it for a while, then decided to contact me, said he didn't want another one of her suckers to suffer as he had, didn't want her to get away with it again.' Tony gestured to his lawyer. 'Show Chloe his statutory declaration.'

The lawyer opened a manila folder and passed her a sheaf of documents. On top was a statutory declaration, made by a John Dennis Flaherty with a Perth address, not anyone she knew or imagined Tony would know since he lived on the other side of Australia. Still, it was entirely possible that newspapers over there had picked up on a juicy celebrity scandal, so that part was credible.

She began reading.

According to John Flaherty, Laura Farrell had been his personal assistant four years ago. She had seductively maneuvred him into a sexual relationship although he loved his wife and had no intention of breaking up his marriage, which he'd made clear to Laura Farrell, who had apparently accepted this situation until she told him she had accidentally fallen pregnant, subsequently pressing him to leave his wife. He refused, ending the affair and offering only to pay support for their child. Laura Farrell went to his wife, begging her to dump him so they could be married. His wife divorced him. He had nothing more to do with Laura Farrell except to pay out a substantial settlement to get her out of his life. A year later he decided he wanted to see his child. He hired a private investigator to track down Laura Farrell. The investigator discovered there was no child and no medical record of there ever being a pregnancy let alone a birth.

Photocopies of the investigator's reports followed. On being questioned, Laura Farrell had declared the money was a personal gift—'a kiss-off'—and there was no proof of anything else. It was her word against his—the ex-wife would not testify on his behalf because he had admitted infidelity—so no legal action for fraud could be taken to recover the money.

It was a nasty story, making Chloe's spine crawl over how Laura had come to her—*the wife*—forcing the marriage break-up then playing on her sympathy, playing every emotional string she could, making herself out to be Tony's victim. Chloe wondered if the substantial settlement had been fifty thousand dollars—not a bad take for a bit of pregnancy padding.

'Laura didn't suck you in, did she?' Tony asked anxiously. 'You didn't shell out a lot of money to her?'

She slowly raised her gaze from the documents to look directly at him. 'No. I thought *you* should. Which is why we're here.'

His face sagged with relief. 'At least she didn't do us that damage.'

It sounded as though he was wiping all fault from himself and Chloe was not about to accept that, eyeing him coldly as she pointed out, 'You put us in this position, Tony. You gave her the power to play this game.'

'Do you think I haven't cursed myself a thousand times for falling into her trap?' he pleaded.

'Laura said you seduced her.'

'Well, she would say that to you, wouldn't she?' he scoffed. 'It served her purpose. Just as it served her purpose to hang out availability signals to me from day one of working for you. Flirtatious looks. Sexy double entendres. The occasional brush past. A whole stack of sly temptations. I laughed it off for months. I didn't want her.'

Again he leaned forward earnestly, his blue eyes begging her understanding. 'I had you, Chloe. I didn't want Laura Farrell. Even when she was doing it to me I told myself I should be stopping her, but I'd had too much to drink at the party and…' He raked his hands through his hair in an anguished manner. 'I tell you, Chloe, she's a female predator. I was coming out of the bathroom. She pushed me back in, had me unzipped in a flash, went down on me and…'

'Spare me the details!' Chloe snapped.

'I'm sorry…sorry… I'm just trying to explain how it was, how I never meant it to happen. I love *you*,' he cried emphatically.

Anger flared at the way he was twisting things again. Whether Laura had seduced him or the other way around didn't really matter because it hadn't stopped in that bathroom. Her eyes savagely mocked any excuse for his continued infidelity.

'Don't tell me this was a once only lapse on your part, Tony. I know it wasn't.'

'What did Laura tell you?' he quickly countered.

Chloe shot down any more lies before he could come up with them. 'My mother told me. She dismissed the affair as unimportant. *The affair*, Tony. Not a one-night stand.'

Chloe could see him recalculating, knowing he was under the gun with Stephanie Rollins's sharp eyes never missing anything. It wouldn't suit her purpose to plead his cause so he had to give the affair a forgivable twist.

'All right,' he conceded with a self-deprecating grimace. 'Laura knew how to work sex to get to me and it did. Any man would have taken what she was giving out. I'm only human, Chloe. But it made me feel guilty as hell and in the end I did stop it because I cared about our marriage and didn't want her messing with it.'

She wondered if Max would have taken what Laura could do with sex. Obviously Tony had found it more exciting than what he'd had at home. Was sex more important to men than love? Perhaps the reason why Max had never married was because sex with the one woman got boring after a while, and he preferred to remain free to go after something new and exciting when the urge took him.

Like with her.

A wave of depression rolled through Chloe. She didn't want to listen to anymore. There was no need to fight for child support on Laura Farrell's behalf. The business of this meeting was over. She looked bleakly at the man she had married with blind faith in love and spoke what she knew to be the truth.

'You didn't want to lose your cash cow, Tony.'

His face flushed an ugly red. 'Those are Laura's words, not mine. She was determined on alienating you from me, Chloe, but she's out of our lives now. No baby for her to hang onto me. That's all behind us.' Again his hands reached out in appeal. 'I'm begging you to forgive me. Give us another chance.'

She shook her head, pushed her chair back and stood up, turning to the two lawyers. 'Thank you for your services in clarifying the situation with Laura Farrell.'

All three men rose to their feet, Tony rushing into more urgent speech. 'Please think about it, Chloe. We had a good marriage before this. I know you wanted a baby and I put it off but I won't if you give us another chance. I promise you…'

Chloe had no doubt he would keep that promise. A baby was the best string of all to hold her to their marriage. But she vividly remembered how he'd treated Luther—a baby dog— and she couldn't see Tony as a good father. Nor as a good husband for her. He never had been.

'This meeting is over,' she stated flatly. 'It wasn't about us, Tony.'

'But surely you now realise I was Laura's victim, just as John Flaherty was,' he pleaded. 'You're letting her win, Chloe.'

'No. She didn't get anything out of this.' Except the five hundred dollars, which would have been peanuts in her over- all scheme.

'She got the satisfaction of breaking us up,' Tony vehemently argued.

Oddly enough, Chloe now felt Laura Farrell had done her a favour—the catalyst for breaking up a lot of bad things in her life. 'I've moved on, Tony. There's no going back,' she said firmly.

An angry red flushed his face this time. 'I can forgive you Max Hart. He took advantage of the situation.'

She shook her head. 'I'm leaving now. I'd appreciate it—' she glanced at Tony's lawyer '—if you and your client remain in this boardroom until I've gone.'

The lawyer nodded. 'Understood, Miss Rollins.'

'Chloe…' Tony persisted pleadingly.

She turned away and her own lawyer escorted her to the door, opening it.

'Max Hart won't marry you,' Tony threw after her. 'He won't give you children. You'll end up on the scrap heap with the rest of the women he's had.'

She knew Max would move on as he always did and she knew it would hurt when he did. But he had been there for her at a critical time in her life, giving her what she needed, helping her to find the strength to become a person who could stand on her own feet and make her own choices. She fiercely resolved to remember the good he'd done after he moved on. It had to outweigh the hurt she would inevitably feel.

Her lawyer stepped back to usher her out of the boardroom. Chloe walked forward into the legal secretary's office.

'I'd give you a better life than Max Hart ever will,' Tony persisted in a last, heart-clawing plea. 'I swear you're the only woman for me. I'll never again even look at anyone else. And we'll have a family. As many children as you want. What we had was good before Laura mucked it up. Think about it, Chloe. Think about it. Call me....'

The door was closed behind her.

Gerry Anderson rose from his chair in the secretary's office.

Chloe thanked her lawyer.

She could leave now and she did.

Max checked his watch again, frowning over the time that had passed since Chloe's eleven o'clock meeting with the lawyers and Tony Lipton.

'What's got you so uptight, Max?' Angus Hilliard inquired, his bespectacled grey eyes glinting with sharp curiosity. 'That's the third time you've checked the time and frowned, apart from the fact you haven't been giving our business your undivided attention.'

Max grimaced at the head of his legal department who was too astute a man to let anything go unnoticed. 'Waiting on a call from Chloe. A bit of nasty stuff going on with Tony Lipton and Laura Farrell.'

'Ah! The pregnant P.A. making more waves? Anything I can do?'

'No. The divorce lawyers are handling it, Angus. What's worrying me is the meeting shouldn't have dragged on this long. I wanted to accompany Chloe to it....'

'Better you didn't, Max.'

'I know. I know. But I don't trust her husband to play anything straight. Anyhow, Chloe came up with the idea of having the security guy escort her to and from the meeting.'

'Gerry Anderson?'

'The same,' Max affirmed.

'He's one of the best,' Angus assured him, having vetted

the security guard personally. 'Why not call him? Check out what's going on? I have his number here.' He opened the teledex on his desk.

'I'm not his client this time,' Max pointed out. 'And Chloe promised to call me.'

'You have his client's interests at heart,' Angus argued. 'I'm sure Anderson will appreciate that position.'

It smacked of going behind Chloe's back. Max didn't like it, yet he felt too uneasy not to make the call. The sense of Chloe separating herself from him was getting stronger. She should have contacted him by now. Unless something was very wrong.

He had to know.

He made the call.

Ten minutes later he was assured that Chloe was safely home, had been since shortly after midday. He'd also been informed of the fraudulent pregnancy—a con game Laura Farrell had played profitably before. The most disturbing news, however, was Gerry Anderson's report of what he'd overheard Tony Lipton say as Chloe was leaving the lawyer's office—the strikes against any hope of sharing a long-term future with him lined up against what her husband was offering. And the final plea...

Call me.

She hadn't made the promised call to him—the man whose lifestyle suggested she was only one link in a chain of many women, none of whom had locked him into marriage or having children.

Was she considering the self-serving promises her husband was holding out to her? Tony Lipton would have played the victim to the hilt, begging forgiveness, pleading for another chance to make a go of their marriage—cancel out his affair with Laura, cancel out her affair with Max, make a fresh start, have a family together...

'Max, you're wearing out my carpet.'

The dry comment jolted him into realising he was prowling around Angus's office like a fiercely frustrated tiger, wanting to lash out at the situation, yet hemmed in by bars he couldn't simply knock aside. Chloe was no longer living on his property, not so readily accessible, especially if she didn't choose to be. And she was still married to Tony Lipton, who was undoubtedly trying to capitilise on Laura Farrell's deceit.

He came to a halt in front of Angus's desk, who leaned back in his chair and held up his hands in mock fear of being shot down where he sat. 'Whoa! I'm not the target. I'm the negotiator, remember? Just point me in the direction you want to take....'

'She's mine!' The words snapped out in an explosive burst of feeling. His hand sliced the air as violently as a slashing sword. 'I don't want that worm of a husband wriggling back into her life!'

Angus shrugged, looking askance at Max as though his behaviour was distinctly weird. 'Why would she take him back?' he queried in a tone of calm reasoning.

Max snarled back at him. 'Because the P.A.'s pregnancy has been proved fraudulent. Because Tony Lipton knows how to twist that to his advantage—an infidelity trade-off—plus all the forever promises of love, having a family.' He threw up his hands. 'That pregnancy was the breaking point because Chloe wanted a baby.'

'Then give her one, Max. Give her one.'

As though it was the simplest thing in the world!

Max rolled his eyes.

Angus proceeded to argue his strategy, the grey eyes glinting absolute certainty behind the frameless spectacles. 'If Chloe wants children, sooner or later you're going to lose her if you're not prepared to give her any. Basic instinct in most women. Given that you want to keep her, there's only one sure-fire *win* position for you to take, Max. Otherwise, you'd best start resigning yourself to letting her go.'

He couldn't bear the thought of letting her go. It would be totally intolerable to watch her walk away from him to share her life with someone else.

Angus wriggled his fingers in a weighing-up gesture. 'You've never had a problem attracting beautiful women. I happen to think that Chloe Rollins has something very special, but…it's your life, Max. Your choice.'

Angus was right.

There was only one sure-fire way to *win*.

The only question was…would Chloe want to join him in the longest run that two people could ever take on together?

CHAPTER FOURTEEN

CHLOE sat on the garden bench in the small backyard, feeding Luther pieces of ham as he frolicked around her feet. It was good to be outside in the open air, good to have the uncomplicated company of her darling little dog. She didn't feel like eating lunch herself yet. The meeting with Tony had left her with a sense of deep distaste. She didn't want to talk about it, either.

Her mobile telephone lay beside her on the bench, along with the mug of coffee she'd brought out to drink. Max would be expecting a call from her. She'd promised to let him know the outcome of the meeting. Dirty business, she thought, the whole thing so horribly grubby she didn't want to rehash it.

Especially the sex in the bathroom bit. Had Max ever had a similar experience while he was in one of his past relationships? Had he knocked it back or let it happen, enjoying the thrill of unplanned pleasure? How much had a woman ever really meant to him, beyond the sexual satisfaction he both took and gave?

She barely registered the distant ringing of the doorbell but Luther went streaking inside to bark at the caller behind the front door. Chloe didn't move, reluctant to see or talk to anyone. It rang a few more times. Luther kept barking. Chloe reasoned that both Gerry Anderson and Max had her mobile telephone number. They could call her to check if she was in or not. No-one else had the right to bother her.

Whoever was at the door eventually went away. Luther returned, looking triumphantly pleased with himself for having driven off what was obviously an unwelcome visitor. He trotted over to her to be petted and she smiled at him, leaning down to pick him up and set him on her lap, where he curled up contentedly as she patted him.

'I'm glad I've got you, Luther,' she murmured—the something *real* Max had given her as a substitute for a baby.

A thoughtful gift.

A caring gift.

But also a stop-gap gift because Max had no intention of giving her a baby.

She realised now why he had commented on her relatively young age—only twenty-seven, not old enough to be desperate about the biological clock. He obviously hadn't wanted to feel guilty about holding up her need for motherhood. Parenthood was not in Max's plans. Lust was a temporary thing in his life, not to be encumbered with any lasting commitment. He'd acted with integrity, but also with self-interest. Which was fair enough, Chloe told herself. It wasn't his fault that she wanted so much more from him.

Luther stirred, his head lifting, ears pricking up, a low growl rumbling in his throat as he stared at the back fence, which closed off the property from a narrow alley between the rows of terrace houses. The gate allowing access to the alley started rattling. Luther leapt off her lap and raced down the yard, barking his head off.

Chloe was stirred to action herself. The gate was bolted so

no-one could gain easy entry, but someone intent on burgling might scale the two-metre fence. Since the front doorbell hadn't been answered, the assumption might well have been made that no-one was home. Breaking in from the backyard was nowhere near as public as from the street along Centennial Park.

She picked up the mobile phone and quickly followed Luther down to the fence. 'I'm calling the police if you don't quit shoving at my gate,' she yelled out. 'Just go away or I'll hit triple zero right now!'

'Chloe!' It sounded like a cry of relief. 'It's me…your mother. I was worried about you. Let me in, for God's sake!'

Chloe was too stunned to reply. Her mother! Here! Who had told her this address? Laura Farrell had tracked it down so it probably wasn't incredible that another determined person could and her mother was nothing if not determined.

'Chloe!' The demanding tone was back in force. 'Let me in!'

'No, I don't think I will,' she answered, bridling against her mother's relentless will-power. 'There's no need to worry about me. I'm perfectly okay.'

'I don't believe it,' her mother snapped. 'You always hid when you were upset about things and that's what you're doing—hiding in there. I can help straighten everything out for you, Chloe. Just open the gate….'

'I don't want your help, Mother. Please go and leave me alone.'

'I know all about the Laura Farrell fraud. I know what went on in your meeting with Tony this morning. He desperately wants you back, Chloe….'

'Have you come as his ambassador?'

'No, of course not! Though I'd have to say he'd be more

devoted to you from now on than Max Hart ever will be, but it's you that I care about. What's best for *you*.'

'I can work that out for myself, thank you.'

'No, you can't. You have no idea. You're a babe in the woods in this business. Max Hart will exploit you for as long as you're starry-eyed with him. You have to understand his interest in you won't last, and if I'm not at your side to make sure there's no fallout damage, you could sink without a trace. If you're clued in you can use this affair with him as a stepping stone. You've got to learn how to use your head, baby! I can teach you, show you how to work the angles…'

Revulsion created waves of nausea through Chloe's empty stomach. The strident voice went on, spelling out how she could *use* Max to advance her career, to extract as much as she could from him while the affair was still running hot, because it would end…

It would end…

'Stop it!' she screamed, unable to bear hearing any more.

'Chloe, this is why you need me,' her mother argued. 'Let me in, baby, so we can talk it through. I'm your mother. I'll always be here for you. You need me.'

'No!' Chloe clapped her hands over her ears. 'I'm going inside now. Leave me be, Mother, or I *will* call the police.'

The voice kept trying to beat at her mind as she bolted away from the fence, almost tripping over Luther, who was scampering around her, distressed at her distress. It was a relief to reach the door into the kitchen, even more of a relief to close herself inside the house. She pelted up the stairs to her bedroom, stripped off her clothes, crawled into bed, buried her face in the pillow and dragged the bed-covers over her head, shutting out the rest of the world and everyone in it.

She didn't care if it was hiding.

Sometimes hiding was the only way to fend off the unbearable.

Max waited for Chloe's call all afternoon, growing more and more tense as the silence from her continued. It wasn't in her nature to break a promise. Had the meeting with Tony stirred such deep mental and emotional turmoil that contacting him felt wrong to her? Whatever was going on, Max couldn't shake the feeling that he was on the losing end of it.

By five o'clock he was determined on confronting the situation. He drove to her house. She didn't answer the doorbell. Luther didn't bark at it, either. It suggested she had gone out and taken the dog with her, possibly for a walk in the park. He crossed the street. It took him half an hour of criss-crossing Centennial Park to assure himself she wasn't there. Totally frustrated at this point, Max whipped out his mobile phone and called her, only to be frustrated further by finding hers was switched off.

He returned to the house, rang the doorbell again. No answer. Chloe had given him a key for his convenience if she was occupied when he arrived at her door. This was not an expected visit and Max was reluctant to use it without her implicit permission. Invasion of privacy did not sit well with him, yet the possibility that something might be badly wrong inside could not be ignored. More accidents occurred in the home than anywhere else.

He unlocked the front door, opened it. As he stepped into the hallway, a low growl alerted him to Luther's presence. He looked up. The dog stood at the top of the stairs, stiff-legged and bristling, ready to leap into attack until he recognised

Max. Then he relaxed and trotted off in the direction of Chloe's bedroom.

Was she asleep? At this hour of the day? Sick? Too ill to move?

Max closed and relocked the door, moved quickly and quietly to the staircase. Conscious of his heart beating much faster than normal, he mounted the stairs two at a time, anxious to check out the situation, do whatever was needed to be done.

She was in bed. Clothes were strewn carelessly around the floor as though getting them off had been her one thought. Only the top of her blonde silky hair was visible above the bed-covers. Her body was tightly curled up beneath them. Luther had nestled himself on the pillow next to hers, obviously intent on being as close as he could, waiting for her face to emerge as well as guarding against her being disturbed.

Max stood beside them for a while, listening to Chloe's breathing. As far as he could tell it was normal. He resisted the urge to strip off his own clothes and join her in bed, not for sex, simply to hold her close and assure himself everything was still right between them. But he knew it wasn't right. She had shut him out. Whether it was a deliberate act or an emotionally fraught one he had no idea. Either way he intended to fight the decision.

He pulled up a chair and sat beside the bed—man and dog both waiting for the most important person in their lives to stir, to respond to them again.

Chloe moved sluggishly towards consciousness. Her eyelids felt too heavy to lift. It was easier to leave them closed. She might slide back into oblivion again. The memory of crying herself to sleep made a blank nothingness more desirable than having her mind recall the reasons for her misery, starting up another tormenting treadmill of thoughts. Better to keep them blocked out.

She took a deep breath and wriggled into a different position, frowning as she realised there was other movement on the bed. Then a small wet tongue licked her forehead. Luther! Had she slept a long time, missing on giving him dinner? It was wrong to keep indulging herself if he was hungry. He'd been such a good guard dog.

She dragged an arm up, pushed the bed-covers away from her head and affectionately ruffled the fur behind Luther's ears. 'It's okay. Mummy's waking up, baby,' she mumbled, slowly forcing her eyes open.

'I'm here, too.'

Max's voice—deep and gravelly, wanting his presence known and acknowledged.

Her eyelids flew up.

He was sitting on a chair beside the bed, leaning forward, elbows on his knees, his dark riveting eyes scanning hers anxiously. 'I was worried about you, Chloe, so I let myself in.'

She grimaced, remembering her promise to call him. 'Sorry. Should have phoned. My mother came and…'

'She came here?'

His sharp concern brought back the whole horrible barrage of advice. 'I won't do it,' she muttered fiercely.

'Do what?'

She hauled herself up to a sitting position, hugging her knees as she viewed the man she loved with rueful eyes, answering his question with blunt honesty. 'Screw all I can get out of you while you're still enjoying a relationship with me.'

He straightened up in his chair, his face tightening with grimly held anger. 'You shouldn't have let her in, Chloe. Shouldn't have listened to her.'

'I didn't let her in. But it's a bit hard not to hear her when she's shouting at you over the back fence.'

'Persistent harridan!' he grated out, rising to his feet, his hand flying out in a furious, cutting-off gesture. 'You can't stay here, Chloe. She's going to keep pestering you now that she knows where you're living. And she'll tell Tony this address, have him camping on your doorstep next, use him to help muddy your mind against me, get you back with her. And him.'

It was strange seeing Max so disturbed and edgy. He'd always been the man in absolute control of himself and the situation. She watched him stalk around her bedroom, aggression pouring from him as he talked through what was on his mind.

'No doubt in the world that Tony won't try to get you back, use Laura Farrell's fraud to plead malevolent manipulation on her part, grovel for forgiveness...'

Surprise spilled into an instant query. 'You know about that?'

He whirled to face her, throwing up his hands in wild dismissal. 'I was worried about you not contacting me. I called Gerry Anderson, and before you say it wasn't my business to ask him what was happening with you, I couldn't stand not knowing if you were in some kind of trouble. Which is also why I used the key you gave me to enter this house when there was no response from you. And Luther showed me where you were because he understands I care about you,' he finished vehemently, his eyes blazing a fierce refusal to accept any protest about his actions.

At the mention of his name, Luther leapt up from his pillow and trotted down to the end of the bed for Max to pat him in approval. Which he did, eyeing Chloe with determined purpose. 'I'm taking you and Luther home with me. No argument.' He took out his mobile phone. 'I'll call Edgar, tell him we're coming, ask Elaine to do dinner for two…'

'No, Max.' She shook her head at him. It was strange how calm she felt, probably from having spent all her emotion before falling asleep this afternoon. 'I'm not going to run away from my life again.'

He frowned. 'You're better off with me. I can protect you, ensure that…'

'For how long, Max?' she wryly inserted.

'As long as need be,' he retorted, his strength of purpose sharp and strong.

She sighed, looking at him with sadly resigned eyes. 'Eventually it will end…whatever you feel for me. And if I let myself become dependent on you, it will be even harder to manage on my own. Today was—' she winced '—difficult…nasty…and I just wanted to shut it out, but I have to face other things that come up, Max, not expect you to always rescue me.'

His mouth thinned in frustration. His eyes burned with the need to override her opposition. 'I don't like it,' burst from him with explosive feeling. 'I don't like you being on your own. You belong with me.'

Belong…?

Her heart flipped at his use of that word. It was the first time he had expressed such a possessive connection—the deep caring it carried. She stared at him, her breathing completely suspended, hopes and fears tumbling through her mind as her need and love for him beat through them, demanding the chance for real fulfilment.

Yet there was one question she wanted answered and it spilled out in a wild rush. 'Would you have had sex with her, Max?'

'What?' He looked stunned, confused.

'Laura Farrell…' A flood of heat burned her cheeks as she explained what she needed to know. 'If she had come onto you in a bathroom…like unzipping you…and…and being aggressively available…'

His grimace held an appalled distaste, wiping the horrid image from her mind even before he spoke a vehement denial. 'Never! I would have knocked her back so fast…' He shook his head, frowning over her need to ask. 'I've been targeted by women like that many times, Chloe. I've always turned them away. They're not only trouble, they're not my choice.'

The relief of absolute certainty was sweet. Of course, Max wouldn't take on anything he didn't choose himself. She should have known that. The formidable drive of the man was based on pursuing *his* will. The master of control. Although he didn't seem so absolutely in control of himself right now.

'Is that how Tony excused his infidelity?' he shot at her, brows beetling down over a dark blaze of anger in his eyes.

'It doesn't matter, Max.'

'It matters to me if you think I'd act like that.'

'No.' She offered an apologetic smile. 'I realise now you wouldn't. I'm sorry for bringing it up.'

'I'm not like Tony, Chloe,' he stated fiercely.

'I know.' She heaved a sigh. 'This whole messy business muddled up my mind.'

'Which is why I want you free of it.' A few quick strides and he was sitting at her side on the bed, one arm curled around her shoulder, turning her towards him, his other hand tenderly caressing her tumbled hair away from her face, his eyes intensely commanding surrender to his will. 'Come home with me, at least for tonight, Chloe. You've had more than enough to deal with today. Let me take you back to Hill House. Let Elaine pamper you with a fine dinner. Give yourself this time to relax and not be hassled by anything.'

He kissed her forehead, as though imprinting his words on her mind. 'Say you will,' he murmured, drawing back enough to give her a self-mocking little smile. 'If only to save me from worrying about you.'

She couldn't help smiling back. 'Well, that's something I can rescue *you* from. So yes, I will. Go ahead and call Edgar while I have a shower and get dressed.'

It was an easy decision to make. Max did care about her and she loved his caring, wanting to bask in it as long as she could. And maybe he would want her to belong with him forever. She had to give it a chance. It was impossible to imagine ever meeting another man as wonderful as him—a man in a million, Maximilian Hart.

CHAPTER FIFTEEN

CHLOE stood under the shower, growing slightly uneasy about her impulsive decision to go with Max to Hill House. It began to feel too much like the beginning of their relationship when she'd taken refuge with him, letting him keep her safe from the same three people who had once again caused her distress. Though she had stood up to them this time—turned them all away from the life she was making for herself. It was really their references to her relationship with Max that had upset her.

But they were wrong about him only wanting her for sexual pleasure. Max cared about her. He'd helped her develop into the more confident person she had become under his guidance—capable of managing by herself, choosing what answered her needs. There was nothing selfish about that. And he worried about her well-being, which surely meant she was much more to him than a throw-away woman who merely served the purpose of satisfying him for a while.

You belong with me now.

Chloe hugged those fiercely spoken words to her heart as she stepped out of the shower, dried herself, and began to get dressed. They felt as though they held a promise that Max would never throw her away. If that was true, letting him take her home with him was okay—a step into a future she hadn't allowed herself to envisage before. Although maybe she was hoping for too much.

Anyway, it was only for one night. The chance that it might mean what she yearned for was worth taking, even though it was going to hurt if it came to nothing apart from removing Max's concern for her.

It wasn't until she automatically checked her appearance in the mirror that she realised her hands had chosen the same blue-and-white polka dot dress she had worn to Hill House the first time Max had taken her there. It shook her for a moment. Was it some psychological slip back into the past?

Then she remembered feeling that electric connection between them when Max had walked into the hotel room and seen her dressed in it. Perhaps it had been more than an unspoken mutual sexual attraction—possibly a subconscious recognition that they would become deeply significant in each other's lives. Chloe wanted to believe that. She kept the dress on, wanting it to be a good omen for the future she couldn't help hoping for.

Having brushed her hair and livened up her face with some make-up, she took a deep breath to settle the nervous flutters in her stomach and walked out of her bedroom to the top of the staircase. Max was in the hallway below, in the act of carrying Luther's transportation basket to the front door, ready to go.

'We don't have to take Luther with us, Max,' she called out. 'He's used to staying here alone when we go to functions.'

He swung around, looking up at her, his dark eyes blazing with determined purpose, battle-tension making his strong, male face all hard angles. 'This isn't a function,' he asserted. Then as he took in her appearance, his expression changed, softening, warming into a smile of pleasure, his eyes transmitting an intense satisfaction that shot a bolt of happiness through Chloe. Clearly she looked *right* to him. Maybe he was even thinking she was right *for* him.

'Luther will be happier with us, Chloe,' he said.

With us…the two of them…the three of them together.

'I've promised him chicken for dinner,' he added persuasively. 'Elaine is already cooking it for him. You know how he loves chicken.'

She laughed, needing some outlet for the bubble of bliss that had bounced around her mind. 'Okay. I can't do him out of that treat,' she replied, telling herself not to attach too much meaning to everything. It would be too big a letdown if she wove a fantasy that had nothing to do with reality.

He watched her walk down the stairs, making her acutely aware of his physical effect on her—the tug that grew stronger with every step she took towards him. He told her he'd locked up the house apart from the front door, which he proceeded to open, ushering her outside. Once they were in his car and on their way, he reached over and took her hand, interlacing his fingers with hers in a strong grip.

Warmth flooded up her arm and tingled through her heart. He wanted connection with her. It definitely wasn't just sexual. She stared down at the physical link he'd just made, not a seductive, sensual one but powerfully possessive, reinforcing those wonderfully sweet words—*you belong with me*.

Please let it be true, Chloe wished, her whole being aching for it to be so. What she had once felt with Tony—being in love—had been such a fluffy, insubstantial thing compared to the depth of her love for Max. She knew there could never be another man to replace him in her life. If he didn't love her as she loved him…but she didn't want to think about that tonight. She simply wanted to soak up all Max's caring for her—caring she'd never had from her mother or Tony.

They arrived at the gates to his property at Vaucluse. He released her hand to operate the remote control to open them. As they drove in and Hill House came into view, a sense of homecoming seared her soul. This was why she had stayed away. It was a magical house with its classical perfection, promising a happy life inside its stately walls. Max had shared it with her. She had loved being here with him.

He parked the car in the courtyard adjacent to the front entrance of the mansion. He didn't immediately alight from the driver's seat, turning to her instead, taking her hand again and studying her face intently as though he needed to see every shade of her response as he said, 'It wasn't only the three E's who've missed having you here, Chloe. I've missed you, too. I hope you feel right about coming back tonight. It feels very right to me.'

For a moment she felt too choked up to speak. His fingers were dragging on the flesh of her hand as though wanting to dig inside her, feel what was going on in her mind and heart and soul. It was impossible to hide how much his words meant to her. She tried not to answer him too fervently.

'Yes, it does feel good, Max. Thank you for…'

'No need to thank me.' He smiled, happy with her reply, his happiness sending hers zooming to giddy heights. 'This house is waiting for you to light it up with your presence. Let's not make it wait any longer.'

She could hardly believe Max saying such a romantic thing to her but she glowed with pleasure at the lovely fantasy that she lit up his home. And he'd missed her being here. Max always spoke the truth. He wasn't into deception. There was no reason not to believe him.

Luther had fallen asleep in his transportation basket. Max lifted it out before collecting her from the passenger seat, offering his arm for the walk up the porch steps. The front door was opened by Edgar before they reached it, the portly butler half-bowing to Max as he stood back to give them entry.

'Good evening, Mr Hart.' Then he actually broke his air of great dignity to smile at Chloe. 'Welcome home, Miss Rollins. We are all delighted to be of service to you again.'

Her heart swelled with a huge rush of emotion. It was so good to be with people who truly liked you and wished you well, no rotten agendas for using you. Her own smile beamed delight back at him. 'Thank you, Edgar. I've missed you, too. And Elaine and Eric. It's lovely to be…here with you all once more,' she finished in a rush.

It had been on the tip of her tongue to say *home*, but as much as she wanted it to be, it wasn't really hers. Not yet. Maybe not ever.

Nevertheless, the three E's went out of their way to make her feel at home. When she and Max took Luther to the kitchen, Elaine fussed over her as though she was a long-lost daughter, Eric was all smiles, saying he'd planted her favourite flowers in pots outside the children's house. Luther woke up and Eric took him out of the basket to give him a cuddle—with much face-licking—exclaiming over how much the little fella had grown and what a good dog he was, great company for when he was working in the grounds.

Edgar served them dinner in the dining room with more panache than usual, encouraging Chloe's appetite by describing in detail the courses Elaine had prepared and informing Max he'd taken the liberty of opening a bottle of his finest wine, which Max instantly approved as entirely appropriate.

Amazingly, Chloe completely relaxed over dinner, basking in the flow of benevolence towards her and the caring implicit in everything Max said and did. The food was superb, the wine divine, and she felt beautifully pampered as though she was very special to everyone at Hill House. And Max's eyes kept telling she was. Which fed the hope that he really meant this to be her home, as well as his.

Not a refuge.

A real home.

For always.

After dinner, he suggested they stroll down to the children's house to check out Eric's flower pots. Daylight saving was still in force so it was only twilight, not too dark to see. She happily agreed, linking her arm with his, loving the feeling of being close to this very special man, wanting the complete sense of intimacy with him.

Max also seemed content to simply have her at his side, remaining silent as they walked around the pool patio. It was a beautiful evening. Stars were appearing in the violet sky. The air was scented with the jasmine that covered some of the pergola. With the northern side of the city lighting up beyond the harbour, it was like looking at a sparkling fairyland over the water.

She smiled to herself, remembering how nervous and wary she'd felt in Max's presence when she'd first come here, disturbed by the sexual magnetism of the man, fearful of his motives for taking her into his protection. He truly cared about her, cared for the person she was and the person she wanted to be. No-one could have looked after her as well as he had, keeping her safe, leading her into thinking for herself, making decisions, acting on them.

She hugged his arm and leaned her head against his shoulder as they descended the flight of steps to the children's terrace. 'Thank you for being the man you are, Max,' she said.

'I'm no longer who I was,' he answered in a wry tone. 'I should be thanking you for the woman you are, Chloe. You've changed the way I've viewed life, made me aware there's far more to be had than what I'd aimed for…settled for…'

'Like what?' she asked, curious to know and understand the effect she'd had on him.

He was slow to reply, and when he did it was as though he was musing to himself, thinking back through the distance of years. 'I guess I learnt emotional detachment from a very early age…the art of a survivor, looking out for myself, not letting other people get to me deeply enough to hurt, not being dependent on anyone for anything. I made myself self-sufficient. That's not to say I haven't enjoyed the company of many people—men and women—but I never let the connection turn into a need for it, because that would have given them a kind of power over me, influencing what I considered the successful operation of my life.'

'Well, no-one could argue with how successful that's been, Max,' she said, her heart catapulting wildly around her chest at the hope he was leading up to saying it was different with her, that the connection between them was so deep, he couldn't bear to live without it.

'Successful as far as ambition and material gain are concerned,' he said mockingly. 'So successful I was blinded to what I was missing.'

They reached the bottom of the steps and started along the

path to the children's house. Chloe wanted to ask what he was missing but Max kept talking and it was more important to listen than to interrupt.

'Even when my instincts were sliding past my mental shield, whispering thoughts that were alien to my usual thinking, I reasoned them away as foolish fantasies.' He shook his head. 'They weren't foolish. Deep down in my heart they were the truth of what I wanted with you, Chloe.'

He stopped her on the doorstep, turned her to face him, his expression gravely intent, his eyes searing hers with a blaze of need. He lifted a hand to her cheek, cupping her face as though it was infinitely precious to him. 'You *are* my Mary.'

Mary? Confusion rolled through Chloe's mind. He'd spoken that name before, when he'd returned to the hotel suite after severing the agency ties with her mother…those few moments of electric stillness as he'd looked at her…then dismissing his use of the name, saying she reminded him of someone.

Anguish twisted through her heart. Had he lost a Mary? She didn't want to be linked to some other woman who'd been dear to him. She needed to be wanted for herself.

'That's not my name, Max,' she whispered hoarsely, her throat having gone completely dry.

'It's *my* name for you. Chloe doesn't suit you. I renamed you Mary in my mind even before there was any chance of our coming together. Not Chloe Rollins. Mary Hart.'

'Hart?' She was so stunned, it was all she could do to mutter, 'But that's your name.'

'Yes. And I'm asking you to take it. Be my wife. Share the rest of your life with me,' he said with a passionate intensity that completely rocked her. 'I know we can't marry until after your divorce but I can't wait another day for us to be together, live together.' He sucked in a deep breath and the words she most yearned to hear burst from his lips. 'I love you, Chloe. I love everything about you. And I want nothing more than for you to be yourself with me.'

'Oh, Max!' The words spilled from her lips on a breath of pure bliss. She wound her arms around his neck, her eyes shining with all the love that didn't have to be hidden anymore. 'I want to be with you, too. All the days of my life. I had to force myself to leave here because I thought there'd be a time limit on our relationship and I had to prepare myself for a separation, even though I knew I'd never love anyone as much as I do you.'

'I hated the separation. We'll never be separated again,' he declared vehemently. 'We'll give each other all we've missed out on in the lives we've had up until now. We'll make the best of all possible futures together, Chloe.'

And he sealed that promise to her in a kiss that made her believe it, the whole indomitable power of the man pouring through her—filling her heart, her mind, her body and soul with absolute trust in him, making her certain that they did belong with each other and always would.

They would have a wonderful future together.

When Maximilian Hart set out to make something happen, he made it happen.

EPILOGUE

VERY shortly after Chloe had accepted Max's proposal of marriage, he informed her that her mother had moved to Los Angeles and would undoubtedly contrive to set up as an actors' agent there. The ruthless gleam in his dark eyes told her the master player had been at work, ensuring that the woman he loved would not be stressed by Stephanie Rollins ever again. Chloe didn't question him about it, simply accepting with huge relief that her mother had been cut completely out of her life and would never re-enter it.

She learnt from her lawyer that Tony had also moved away from Sydney, setting himself up at Byron Bay on the far north coast of New South Wales where there was a community of writers. Apparently he fancied the idea of writing a book. Chloe thought it more likely that was an image he would use to pass himself off as someone worth knowing while he bummed around on her money.

Not that she cared. It was worth the divorce settlement to have him out of sight and out of mind. She wondered if Max had forcefully suggested the move to him but he only muttered, 'Good riddance!' when she passed on the news. The divorce went through without any further meeting with Tony and that, also, was a relief.

Chloe did not worry about being confronted by Laura Farrell again. Her ex-P.A. would have known her fraud would be uncovered as soon as Tony was contacted about child support, making it certain there was no profit in making another approach. She was, in fact, arrested some months later, for trying to blackmail a prominent businessman, and Chloe was glad that someone had put an end to her evil mischief.

She and Max were married as soon as it was legally possible.

Gerry Anderson became a permanent fixture in their lives, accompanying Chloe whenever Max could not be at her side, and watching out for their children's safety as the years went on.

Max moved on to producing movies, which always starred his wife and were invariably box-office successes because he never chose to bring anything but satisfying stories to the big screen. The two of them became legends in the movie world, renowned not only for having the golden touch, but for being a golden couple, their obvious love for each other never losing its shine.

They had four children, two boys and two girls, all of whom travelled with them wherever they went. They had residences in New York and London, villas in France and Italy, but these were only places for their family to live when work demanded they be in other countries. Hill House was always home to them.

The children loved having their own little house to play in and it was kept for their exclusive use. Guests were housed in the mansion. The three E's stayed on, keeping everything as it should be for the rest of their lives, training and supervising their replacements as they grew too old to carry on their roles themselves. They were like grandparents, enjoying and taking a caring interest in the children, minding Luther when the family was away.

Luther lived to the grand old age of eighteen. He was buried beside the children's house with a gravestone that read Here lies Luther, the best guard dog in the world, and much loved pet of the Hart family.

The question Max had once asked of himself—would he be good for Chloe Rollins in the long run?—lost all significance in the future they made together. He took immense pleasure in watching her face show everything she felt and those feelings invariably lifted his own heart. He was not only good for her, she was good for him.

He didn't know that in her eyes he was her wonderful white knight.

Not one bit dark.

He'd banished all the darkness for her, just as she had for him.

In their private life they became known as Max and Mary to all those close to them.

HARLEQUIN *Presents*

Bestselling Harlequin Presents author

Lynne Graham

brings you an exciting new miniseries:

PREGNANT BRIDES

Inexperienced and expecting, they're forced to marry

Collect them all:

DESERT PRINCE, BRIDE OF INNOCENCE
January 2010

RUTHLESS MAGNATE, CONVENIENT WIFE
February 2010

GREEK TYCOON, INEXPERIENCED MISTRESS
March 2010

www.eHarlequin.com

HP12884

REQUEST YOUR FREE BOOKS!

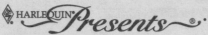 HARLEQUIN *Presents*®

2 FREE NOVELS PLUS 2 FREE GIFTS!

PASSION GUARANTEED SEDUCTION

YES! Please send me 2 FREE Harlequin Presents® novels and my 2 FREE gifts (gifts are worth about $10). After receiving them, if I don't wish to receive any more books, I can return the shipping statement marked "cancel." If I don't cancel, I will receive 6 brand-new novels every month and be billed just $4.05 per book in the U.S. or $4.74 per book in Canada. That's a savings of close to 15% off the cover price! It's quite a bargain! Shipping and handling is just 50¢ per book*. I understand that accepting the 2 free books and gifts places me under no obligation to buy anything. I can always return a shipment and cancel at any time. Even if I never buy another book, the two free books and gifts are mine to keep forever.

106 HDN EYRQ 306 HDN EYR2

Name	(PLEASE PRINT)	
Address		Apt. #
City	State/Prov.	Zip/Postal Code

Signature (if under 18, a parent or guardian must sign)

Mail to the **Harlequin Reader Service:**
IN U.S.A.: P.O. Box 1867, Buffalo, NY 14240-1867
IN CANADA: P.O. Box 609, Fort Erie, Ontario L2A 5X3

Not valid to current subscribers of Harlequin Presents books.

Are you a current subscriber of Harlequin Presents books and want to receive the larger-print edition? Call 1-800-873-8635 today!

* Terms and prices subject to change without notice. Prices do not include applicable taxes. Sales tax applicable in N.Y. Canadian residents will be charged applicable provincial taxes and GST. Offer not valid in Quebec. This offer is limited to one order per household. All orders subject to approval. Credit or debit balances in a customer's account(s) may be offset by any other outstanding balance owed by or to the customer. Please allow 4 to 6 weeks for delivery. Offer available while quantities last.

Your Privacy: Harlequin Books is committed to protecting your privacy. Our Privacy Policy is available online at www.eHarlequin.com or upon request from the Reader Service. From time to time we make our lists of customers available to reputable third parties who may have a product or service of interest to you. If you would prefer we not share your name and address, please check here. ☐

HP09R

I ♥ HARLEQUIN® Presents

BROUGHT TO YOU BY FANS OF HARLEQUIN PRESENTS.

We are its editors and authors and biggest fans—and we'd love to hear from YOU!

Subscribe today to our online blog at www.iheartpresents.com